Santa Monica Public Library

I SMP 00 2656792 1

D1443295

FAIRVIEW BRANCH
Santa Monica Public Library

NOV - - 2016

FANTASTIC BEASTS
AND WHERE TO FIND THEM

THE
ORIGINAL SCREENPLAY

J.K. ROWLING'S · WIZARDING WORLD · WW

J.K. ROWLING

FANTASTIC BEASTS
AND WHERE TO FIND THEM™

THE ORIGINAL SCREENPLAY

ILLUSTRATIONS AND DESIGN
BY
MINALIMA

ARTHUR A. LEVINE BOOKS
AN IMPRINT OF SCHOLASTIC INC.

Text copyright © 2016 by J.K. Rowling
Illustrations by MinaLima © 2016 by J.K. Rowling
Harry Potter and Fantastic Beasts Publishing Rights © J.K. Rowling
HARRY POTTER and FANTASTIC BEASTS characters, names, and related indicia are
trademarks of and © Warner Bros. Entertainment Inc. All Rights Reserved.
J.K. ROWLING'S WIZARDING WORLD is a trademark of J.K. Rowling and Warner Bros.
Entertainment Inc.

All rights reserved. Published by Arthur A. Levine Books, an imprint of Scholastic Inc.,
Publishers since 1920. SCHOLASTIC and the LANTERN LOGO are trademarks and/or registered
trademarks of Scholastic Inc.

The publisher does not have any control over and does not assume any responsibility for
author or third-party websites or their content.

No part of this publication may be reproduced, stored in a retrieval system, or transmitted
in any form or by any means, electronic, mechanical, photocopying, recording, or
otherwise, without written permission of the publisher. For information regarding
permission, write to Scholastic Inc., Attention: Permissions Department, 557 Broadway,
New York, NY 10012.

This book is a work of fiction. Names, characters, places, and incidents are either the
product of the author's imagination or are used fictitiously, and any resemblance to actual
persons, living or dead, business establishments, events, or locales is entirely coincidental.
Library of Congress Control Number Available

ISBN 978-1-338-13208-3

10 9 8 7 6 5 4 3 2 1   16 17 18 19 20

Printed in the U.S.A. at LSC Communications, Crawfordsville, Indiana
Library edition, November 2016

MIX
Paper from
responsible sources
FSC   FSC® C132124
www.fsc.org

We try to produce the most beautiful books possible, and we are also extremely concerned
about the impact of our manufacturing process on the forests of the world and
the environment as a whole. Accordingly, we made sure that all of the paper we used
contains 30% post-consumer recycled fiber and has been certified as coming from
forests that are managed to insure the protection of the people and wildlife dependent
upon them.

To the memory of Gordon Murray,
real-life creature healer and hero

CONTENTS

SCENE 1
EXT. SOMEWHERE IN EUROPE—1926—NIGHT

A large, isolated, derelict chateau emerges from the darkness. We focus on a cobbled square outside the building, shrouded in mist, eerie, silent.

Five Aurors stand, wands aloft, tentative as they edge toward the chateau. A sudden explosion of pure white light sends them flying.

We whip around to find their bodies scattered, lying motionless at the entrance to a large parkland. A figure (Grindelwald) enters the frame, his back to the camera; ignoring the bodies, he stares out into the night sky as we pan up toward the moon.

MONTAGE:

We see various magical newspaper headlines from 1926 relating to Grindelwald's attacks all over the world:
GRINDELWALD STRIKES AGAIN IN EUROPE, HOGWARTS SCHOOL

INCREASES SECURITY, ANTI-WIZARD FEELING ON THE RISE, WHERE IS GRINDELWALD?, IS ANYONE SAFE? He's a serious threat to the magical community and he's vanished. Moving photos detail destroyed buildings, fires, screaming victims. The articles come thick and fast—the worldwide hunt for Grindelwald continues. We push in on a final article displaying the Statue of Liberty.

TRANSITION TO:

SCENE 2
EXT. SHIP GLIDING INTO NEW YORK—NEXT MORNING

A bright, clear New York day. Seagulls swoop overhead.

A large passenger ship glides past the Statue of Liberty. Passengers lean over the rails, looking excitedly toward the oncoming land.

We push in toward a figure sitting on a bench with his back to us—Newt Scamander, weather-beaten, wiry, wearing an old blue overcoat. Beside him rests a battered brown leather case. A catch on the case flicks open of its own accord. Newt swiftly bends down to close it.

Placing the case on his lap, Newt leans in, whispering:

NEWT
Dougal—you settle down
now, please. It won't be long.

SCENE 3
EXT. NEW YORK—DAY

AERIAL SHOT of New York.

SCENE 4
EXT. SHIP/INT. CUSTOMS—SHORTLY
AFTERWARD—DAY

*Among bustling crowds, Newt walks down the gangplank
of the ship as we push in toward his case.*

CUSTOMS OFFICIAL (O.S.)
Next.

*Newt stands at customs—a long row of desks by the
shipyard, manned by serious-looking American officials.
A customs official examines Newt's very tattered British
passport.*

CUSTOMS OFFICIAL
British, huh?

NEWT
Yes.

CUSTOMS OFFICIAL
First trip to New York?

NEWT
Yes.

CUSTOMS OFFICIAL
(*gesturing to Newt's case*)
Anything edible in there?

NEWT
(*placing a hand over his
breast pocket*)
No.

CUSTOMS OFFICIAL
Livestock?

The catch on Newt's case flicks open again. Newt looks down and hastily closes it.

NEWT
Must get that fixed—ahh, no.

CUSTOMS OFFICIAL
(suspicious)
Let me take a look.

Newt places the case on the desk between them and discreetly flicks a brass dial to MUGGLEWORTHY.

The customs official spins the case toward him and pops the catches, lifting the lid to reveal:

Pajamas, various maps, a journal, an alarm clock, a magnifying glass, and a Hufflepuff scarf. Finally satisfied, he closes the case.

CUSTOMS OFFICIAL
Welcome to New York.

NEWT
Thank you.

Newt gathers his passport and case.

CUSTOMS OFFICIAL
Next!

Newt exits through customs.

SCENE 5
EXT. STREET NEAR CITY HALL SUBWAY—
DUSK

*A long street of identical brownstone houses, one of which
has been reduced to rubble. A gaggle of reporters and
photographers mills around in the vague hope of something
happening, but without much enthusiasm. One reporter is
interviewing an excitable middle-aged man as they move
through the rubble.*

> WITNESS
> —and it was like a—like a
> *wind* or like a—like a *ghost*—
> but dark—and I saw its eyes—
> shinin' white eyes—

> REPORTER
> *(expressionless—notebook*
> *in his hand)*
> —a dark wind—with eyes . . .

> WITNESS
> —like a dark *mass*, and it
> dove down there, down
> underground—I swear to
> God . . . into the earth right in
> front of me.

CLOSE ON PERCIVAL GRAVES as he walks toward the destroyed building.

Graves: smart clothing, very handsome, early middle-age, his demeanor differs from those around him. He is watchful, tightly coiled, an air of intense confidence.

> PHOTOGRAPHER
> *(sotto voce)*
> Hey—did you get anything?

REPORTER
(*sotto voce*)
Dark wind, blah blah.

PHOTOGRAPHER
It's some atmospheric hooey.
Or electrical.

Graves moves up the steps of the now ruined building. He examines the destruction, curious, alert.

REPORTER
Hey—you thirsty?

PHOTOGRAPHER
Nah, I'm on the wagon.
Promised Martha I'd lay off.

Wind begins to pick up, swirling around the building, accompanied by a high-pitched screeching. Graves alone looks interested.

A sudden series of bangs at street level. All turn to look for the source of the sound: A wall cracks, the rubble on the floor begins to shake before exploding like an earthquake, ripping out of the building and down through the middle of the street. The movement is violent, rushed—people and cars go flying.

The mysterious force then flies up into the air, swirling

through the city, diving in and out of alleyways, before crashing down into a subway station.

CLOSE ON GRAVES as he examines the destruction of the street.

A mingled roar and howl emanates from the bowels of the earth.

SCENE 6
EXT. NEW YORK STREET—DAY

Watching Newt walk, we see in him an unselfconscious Keatonesque quality, a sense of a different rhythm to those around him. In his hand he clutches directions on a small piece of paper, but still shows a scientist's curiosity about this alien environment.

SCENE 7
EXT. ANOTHER STREET, STEPS OF THE CITY BANK—DAY

Newt, intrigued by the noise of shouting, approaches a rally of the New Salem Philanthropic Society.

Mary Lou Barebone, a handsome midwestern woman in a 1920s version of Puritan dress, charismatic and earnest, stands on a small stage at the steps to the City Bank.

Behind her stands a man parading a banner emblazoned with the organization's symbol: hands proudly grasping a broken wand amid bright yellow and red flames.

> MARY LOU
> *(to the assembled crowd)*
> . . . this great city sparkles
> with the jewels of man's
> invention! Movie theaters,
> automobiles, the wireless,
> electric lights—all dazzle and
> bewitch us!

Newt slows down and watches Mary Lou as he would observe a foreign species: no judgment, simply interest.

Nearby stands Tina Goldstein, hat low on her head, upturned collar. She is eating a hot dog, mustard smeared

*on her upper lip. Newt accidentally bumps into her as he
makes his way to the front of the rally.*

> NEWT
> Oh . . . so sorry.

> MARY LOU
> But where there is light there
> is shadow, friend. Something
> is stalking our city, wreaking
> destruction and then disap-
> pearing without a trace . . .

*Jacob Kowalski moves nervously down the street toward
the crowd, wearing an ill-fitting brown suit and carrying a
battered brown leather case.*

> MARY LOU (O.S.)
> We have to fight—join us, the
> Second Salemers, in our fight!

*Jacob makes his way through the gathered crowds, also
pushing past Tina.*

> JACOB
> Excuse me, doll, just trying to
> get to the bank—excuse me—
> just trying . . .

*Jacob trips over Newt's case, disappearing momentarily.
Newt hauls him up.*

NEWT
I'm so sorry—my case—

JACOB
No harm done—

Jacob struggles on, heading past Mary Lou and up the steps of the bank.

JACOB
Excuse me!

The kerfuffle around Newt draws Mary Lou's attention.

MARY LOU
(charming, to Newt)
You, friend! What drew you
to our meeting today?

Newt is startled to find himself the center of attention.

NEWT
Oh . . . I was just—passing . . .

MARY LOU
Are you a seeker? A seeker
after truth?

A beat.

> NEWT
> I'm more of a chaser, really.

ANGLE ON PEOPLE moving in and out of the bank.

A smartly dressed man flips a dime toward a beggar sitting on the steps.

CLOSE ON THE DIME, falling in slow motion.

> MARY LOU (O.S.)
> Hear my words and heed my
> warning . . .

ANGLE ON SOME LITTLE PAWS, which have appeared in the narrow crack between the lid and the body of Newt's case.

ANGLE ON THE DIME hitting the steps with a musical clang.

ANGLE ON THE PAWS, now trying hard to prize open the case.

> MARY LOU
> . . . and laugh if you dare:
> *Witches live among us!*

Mary Lou's three adopted children, adults Credence and

Chastity, and Modesty (an eight-year-old girl), hand out leaflets. Credence appears nervous and troubled.

> MARY LOU (O.S.)
> We have to fight together for
> the sake of our children—for
> the sake of tomorrow!
> *(to Newt)*
> What do you say to that,
> friend?

As Newt looks up toward Mary Lou, something seen from the corner of his eye catches his attention. The Niffler, a small, furry black cross between a mole and a duck-billed platypus, is sitting on the steps of the bank, hastily pulling the beggar's hat full of money out of sight behind a pillar.

Newt, startled, looks down at his case.

ANGLE ON THE NIFFLER, busy shoveling the beggar's coins into a pouch in its belly. The Niffler looks up, notices Newt's gaze, and hurriedly gathers the rest of the coins before tumbling away and into the bank.

Newt jolts forward.

> NEWT
> Excuse me.

ANGLE ON MARY LOU—she looks confused at Newt's lack of interest in her cause.

> MARY LOU (O.S.)
> Witches live among us.

ANGLE ON TINA, moving through the crowds, eyeing Newt suspiciously.

SCENE 8
INT. LOBBY OF BANK—MOMENTS LATER—DAY

A large, impressive-looking bank atrium. In the center, behind a golden counter, clerks are busy at work serving customers.

Newt skids to a halt in the entrance of the space and looks around to find his creature. His dress and demeanor make him out of place among the smartly dressed New Yorkers.

> BANK EMPLOYEE
> *(suspicious)*
> Can I help you, sir?

> NEWT
> No, I was just . . . just . . .
> waiting . . .

Newt motions toward a bench and backs away, taking a seat next to Jacob.

Tina peers at Newt from behind a pillar.

JACOB
(nervous)
Hi. What brings you here?

Newt is desperately trying to spot his Niffler.

NEWT
Same as you . . .

JACOB
You're here to get a loan to
open up a bakery?

NEWT
*(looking around—
preoccupied)*
Yes.

JACOB
What are the odds of that?
Well, may the best man win,
I guess.

Newt spots the Niffler, which is now stealing coins from someone's bag.

Jacob holds out his hand, but Newt is off.

> NEWT
> Excuse me.

Newt darts away. In his place on the bench lies a large silver egg.

> JACOB
> Hey, mister . . . Hey, mister!

Newt doesn't hear; he is too engaged in hunting the Niffler.

Jacob picks up the egg just as the door into the bank manager's office opens, and a secretary looks out.

> JACOB
> Hey, fella!

> SECRETARY
> Mr. Kowalski, Mr. Bingley
> will see you now.

Pocketing the egg, Jacob heads toward the office, steeling himself.

> JACOB
> *(under his breath)*
> Okay . . . Okay.

ANGLE ON NEWT, surreptitiously pursuing the Niffler as it moves through the bank. He finally spots it removing a glittering buckle from a lady's shoe before scurrying onward, eager for more shiny objects.

As Newt watches, helpless, the Niffler jumps lithely between cases and into bags, snatching and pilfering.

SCENE 9
INT. BINGLEY'S OFFICE—MOMENTS LATER—DAY

Jacob is facing the imposing and impeccably suited Mr. Bingley. Bingley is examining Jacob's business proposal for a bakery.

An uncomfortable silence. The sound of a ticking clock and Bingley murmuring.

Jacob looks down at his pocket—the egg has started to vibrate.

> BINGLEY
> You are currently working . . .
> in a canning factory?

> JACOB
> That's the best I can do—I
> only got back in '24.

> BINGLEY
> Got back?

> JACOB
> From Europe, sir. Yeah—I
> was part of the Expeditionary
> Forces there—

Jacob is clearly nervous, miming a digging action to the words "Expeditionary Forces," in the vain hope that a joke might help his cause.

SCENE 10
INT. BACK ROOM OF THE BANK—MOMENTS LATER—DAY

We cut back to Newt in the bank—in seeking the Niffler, he has ended up waiting in line for a bank teller. He cranes his neck, peering toward the bag of a lady at the front of the line. Tina watches him from behind a pillar.

ANGLE ON COINS spilling from underneath a bench.

ANGLE ON NEWT, who hears the coins and turns to see small paws hastily gathering them up.

ANGLE ON THE NIFFLER sitting under the bench, looking fat and smug. Not yet satisfied, its attention is caught by the shiny tag hanging around the neck of a small dog. The Niffler moves slowly, cheekily, forward—little paw outstretched to grab the tag. The dog snarls and barks.

Newt starts forward and dives under the bench—the Niffler runs, scuttling over the bank counter screens and out of Newt's reach.

SCENE 11
INT. BINGLEY'S OFFICE—MOMENTS LATER—DAY

Jacob opens his case with great pride. Inside is displayed a selection of his homemade pastries.

JACOB (O.S.)
All right.

> BINGLEY
Mr. Kowalski—

> JACOB
—You gotta try the paczki,
okay, it's my grandmother's
recipe, the orange zest—just—

Jacob holds out a paczki . . . Bingley is not distracted.

> BINGLEY
Mr. Kowalski, what do you
propose to offer the bank as
collateral?

> JACOB
Collateral?

> BINGLEY
Collateral.

Jacob gestures hopefully toward his pastries.

> BINGLEY
There are machines now that
can produce hundreds of
doughnuts an hour—

JACOB
I know, I know, but they're
nothing like what I can do—

BINGLEY
The bank must be protected,
Mr. Kowalski. Good day to
you.

Bingley dismissively rings a bell on his desk.

SCENE 12
INT. BEHIND THE BANK COUNTERS—
MOMENTS LATER—DAY

*The Niffler sits on a trolley covered in money bags, which
it greedily empties into its pouch. As Newt watches through
the security bars, aghast, a guard pushes the trolley away
down a corridor.*

SCENE 13
INT. BINGLEY'S BANK, HALL—MOMENTS
LATER—DAY

Jacob, downcast, exits Bingley's office. His bulging pocket vibrates. Alarmed, he pulls out the egg and looks around.

ANGLE ON THE NIFFLER, still sitting on the trolley, which is now being pushed into an elevator.

ANGLE ON JACOB, who sees Newt in the distance.

> JACOB
> Hey, Mr. English guy! I think
> your egg is hatching.

Newt looks hurriedly between Jacob and the shutting elevator doors before making a decision: He points his wand at Jacob. Jacob and the egg are pulled magically across the bank atrium toward Newt. In a split second, they Disapparate.

Tina stares, incredulous, from behind a pillar.

SCENE 14
INT. BACK ROOM OF THE BANK/STAIRCASE—DAY

Newt and Jacob Apparate into a narrow stairwell leading to the bank's vaults, suddenly past the tellers and security guards.

Newt gently takes the egg back from Jacob as it hatches, revealing a small, blue, snake-like bird—an Occamy. Newt, his face full of wonder, looks to Jacob as though expecting a similar reaction from him.

Slowly, Newt carries the baby creature down the stairs.

> JACOB
> Excuse me . . .

Jacob, very confused, looks back up the stairs toward the main bank atrium. On seeing Bingley approaching, he ducks down the stairs, out of sight.

> JACOB
> *(to himself)*
> I was—over there. I was—
> over there?

SCENE 15
INT. BASEMENT CORRIDOR OF BANK,
LEADING TO VAULT—DAY

*JACOB'S POV—Newt is crouched down, opening his case.
He carefully places the hatched Occamy inside, whispering
tenderly:*

> NEWT
> In you hop . . .

> JACOB (O.S.)
> Hello?

> NEWT
> No. Everyone settle down—
> stay. Dougal, don't make me
> come in there . . .

Jacob moves along the corridor, staring at Newt.

*We see a strange green creature, part stick insect, part
plant, poke its head out of Newt's breast pocket, intrigued.
This is Pickett, a Bowtruckle.*

NEWT
Don't make me come down
there.

*Newt looks up to see the Niffler squeezing itself through
locked doors, into the central vault.*

NEWT
Absolutely not!

Newt takes out his wand and points it at the vault.

NEWT
Alohomora.

We watch the locks and cogs of the vault door turn.

*Bingley comes around the corner, just as the vault door
starts to open.*

BINGLEY
(to Jacob)
Oh, so you're gonna STEAL
the money, huh?

*Bingley hits a button on the wall. An alarm sounds. Newt
aims his wand . . .*

NEWT
Petrificus Totalus!

Bingley suddenly stiffens and falls back flat on the ground. Jacob cannot believe his eyes.

> JACOB
>
> Mr. Bingley!

The vault door opens wide.

> MR. BINGLEY
> *(in his paralyzed state)*
> . . . Kowalski!

Newt hurries into the vault. Inside he finds the Niffler lying among hundreds of opened deposit boxes, and seated on a great pile of cash. The Niffler stares at Newt defiantly as it forces another gold bar into its already overflowing pouch.

> NEWT
>
> Really?!

Newt grasps the Niffler tightly and turns it upside down, shaking it by its hind legs. An extraordinary, and seemingly endless, number of precious items fall out.

> NEWT
> *(to the Niffler)*
> No . . .

Jacob looks around him in disbelief, an almost queasy fear.

Despite their altercation, Newt is fond of the Niffler. He grins as he tickles its stomach, causing more treasure to pour out.

Footsteps on the stairs as several armed guards run down and into the vault corridor.

> JACOB
> *(panicking)*
> Oh no . . . No . . . Don't shoot.
> Don't shoot!

Newt quickly seizes Jacob, and the two of them, plus the Niffler and case, Disapparate.

SCENE 16
EXT. DESERTED SIDE STREET NEXT TO THE BANK—DAY

Newt and Jacob Apparate onto a side street. Security alarms ring out from the bank and, at the end of the side street, we see crowds gathering, police arriving.

Tina runs out of the bank and looks down. She sees Newt

wrestling the Niffler back into the case, Jacob cowering by a wall.

                    JACOB
          Ahhh!

                    NEWT
          For the last time, you
          pilfering pest—paws off what
          doesn't belong to you!

Newt shuts his case, then looks around at Jacob.

                    NEWT
          I'm awfully sorry about all
          that—

                    JACOB
          What the *hell* was that?

                    NEWT
          Nothing that need concern
          you. Now unfortunately you
          have seen far too much, so if
          you wouldn't mind—if you
          just stand there—this will be
          over in a jiffy.

Newt, trying to find his wand, turns his back on Jacob.
Jacob takes the opportunity, seizes his case, swinging it
violently at Newt, who is knocked to the ground.

JACOB

Sorry—

Jacob runs for his life.

Newt holds his head for a moment and looks after Jacob, who
has hurried down the alleyway and into the crowd.

NEWT

Bugger!

Tina comes walking down the side street with purpose.
Newt gathers himself, picks up the case, and, trying to be
nonchalant, walks toward her. As he passes her, Tina grabs
Newt's elbow and Disapparates.

SCENE 17
EXT. NARROW ALLEYWAY OPPOSITE BANK—DAY

Newt and Tina Apparate into a cramped, bricked-up alleyway. We can still hear police sirens sounding in the background.

Tina, incredulous and out of breath, rounds on Newt:

> TINA
>
> Who *are* you?

> NEWT
>
> I'm sorry?

> TINA
>
> Who *are you?*

> NEWT
>
> Newt Scamander. And you are?

> TINA
>
> What's that *thing* in your case?

> NEWT
>
> That's my Niffler.
> (*pointing at hot dog mustard still on Tina's lip*)

Er, you've got something on
your—

TINA
Why in the name of
Deliverance Dane did you let
that thing loose?

NEWT
I didn't mean to—he's
incorrigible, you see,
anything shiny, he's all over
the place—

TINA
You didn't mean to?

NEWT
No.

TINA
You could not have chosen
a worse time to let that
creature loose! We're in the
middle of a situation here! I'm
taking you in.

NEWT
You're taking me where?

She produces her official ID card. It bears her moving picture and an impressive symbol of an American eagle: MACUSA.

> TINA
> Magical Congress of the
> United States of America.

> NEWT
> *(nervous)*
> So, you work for MACUSA?
> What are you, some kind of
> investigator?

> TINA
> *(hesitates)*
> Uh-huh.

She stuffs her identification card back into her coat.

> TINA
> Can you please tell me you
> took care of the No-Maj?

> NEWT
> The what?

> TINA
> *(becoming irritated)*
> The No-Maj! No-magic—the
> non-wizard!

NEWT

Oh, sorry, we call them
Muggles.

TINA
(*getting really worried*)
You wiped his memory,
right? The No-Maj with the
case?

NEWT

Um . . .

TINA
(*appalled*)
That's a Section 3A, Mr.
Scamander. I'm taking you in.

She takes Newt by the arm and they Disapparate again.

SCENE 18
EXT. BROADWAY—DAY

An ornately carved, incredibly tall skyscraper on the corner of a bustling street—the Woolworth Building.

Newt and Tina hurry along Broadway toward this building, Tina almost dragging Newt by his coat sleeve.

> TINA
> Come on.

> NEWT
> Er—sorry, but I do have
> things to do, actually.

TINA
Well, you'll have to rearrange
them!

Tina forcefully guides Newt through the busy traffic.

TINA
What are you doing in New
York anyway?

NEWT
I came to buy a birthday
present.

TINA
Couldn't you have done that
in London?

They have arrived outside the Woolworth Building.
Workers move in and out of a large revolving door.

NEWT
No, there's only one breeder
of Appaloosa Puffskeins in
the world and he lives in New
York, so no . . .

Tina moves Newt toward a side door, guarded by a man in
a cloaked uniform.

TINA
(to the guard)
I got a Section 3A.

The guard immediately opens the door.

SCENE 19
INT. WOOLWORTH BUILDING RECEPTION—
DAY

A normal 1920s office atrium, people milling around and chatting.

TINA (O.S.)
Hey. By the way, we closed
that guy down a year ago.
We don't allow the breeding
of magical creatures in New
York.

We pan around and watch Tina come through the door with Newt. As they enter, the whole entrance magically transforms from the Woolworth Building to the Magical Congress of the United States of America (MACUSA).

SCENE 20
INT. MACUSA LOBBY—DAY

NEWT'S POV—They move up a wide staircase and enter the main lobby—a vast, impressive space with impossibly high vaulted ceilings.

High up—a gigantic dial with many cogs and faces emblazoned with the legend: MAGICAL EXPOSURE THREAT LEVEL. *The hand on the dial points to* SEVERE: UNEXPLAINED ACTIVITY. *Behind it hangs an imposing portrait of a majestic-looking witch: Seraphina Picquery, MACUSA president.*

Owls circulate, witches and wizards in 1920s dress are hard at work. Tina guides an impressed-looking Newt through the bustle. They pass several wizards sitting in a line, waiting to have their wands shined by a house-elf who operates a complex contraption of feathers.

Newt and Tina reach an elevator. The doors open to reveal Red, a goblin bellboy.

RED

Hey, Goldstein.

TINA

Hey, Red.

Tina pushes Newt inside.

SCENE 21
INT. ELEVATOR—DAY

TINA
(to Red)
Major Investigation
Department.

RED
I thought you was—

TINA
*Major Investigation
Department!* I got a
Section 3A!

*Red uses a long clawed stick to reach an elevator button
above his head. The elevator descends.*

SCENE 22
INT. MAJOR INVESTIGATION DEPARTMENT—DAY

CLOSE ON A NEWSPAPER—The New York Ghost, *with the headline* MAGICAL DISTURBANCES RISK WIZARDING EXPOSURE.

A group of the highest-level Aurors in the organization are gathered together in serious discussion. Among them is Graves, examining the newspaper, his face cut and bruised from last night's encounter with the strange entity, and President Seraphina Picquery herself.

> MADAM PICQUERY
> The International Confeder-
> ation is threatening to send
> a delegation. They think this
> is related to Grindelwald's
> attacks in Europe.

> GRAVES
> I was there. This is a beast.
> No human could do what this
> thing is capable of, Madam
> President.

MADAM PICQUERY (O.S.)
Whatever it is, one thing's
clear—it must be stopped.
It's terrorizing No-Majs and
when No-Majs are afraid,
they attack. This could mean
exposure. It could mean war.

On hearing footsteps, the group looks around to see Tina,
who approaches cautiously, leading Newt.

MADAM PICQUERY
(angry but contained)
I made your position here
quite clear, Miss Goldstein.

TINA
(frightened)
Yes, Madam President, but
I—

MADAM PICQUERY
You are no longer an Auror.

TINA
No, Madam President, but—

MADAM PICQUERY
Goldstein.

> TINA
> There's been a minor
> incident—

> MADAM PICQUERY
> Well, this office is currently
> concerned with very major
> incidents. Get out.

> TINA
> *(humiliated)*
> Yes, ma'am.

Tina pushes a bemused-looking Newt back toward the elevator. Graves looks after them, the only one to appear sympathetic.

SCENE 23
INT. BASEMENT—DAY

The elevator descends rapidly through the long elevator shaft.

The doors open onto a cramped, airless, windowless

basement room. A painful contrast to the floor above.
Clearly the place where utter no-hopers work.

Tina leads Newt past a hundred typewriters clacking away
unmanned with a tangle of glass pipes hanging down from
the ceiling above them.

As each memo or form is completed by a typewriter, it folds
itself into an origami rat, which scurries up the appropriate
tube to the offices above. Two rats collide and fight, tearing
each other apart.

Tina walks toward a dingy corner of the room. A sign:
WAND PERMIT OFFICE.

Newt ducks under it.

SCENE 24
INT. WAND PERMIT OFFICE—DAY

The Wand Permit Office is only slightly larger than a
cupboard. There are piles of unopened wand applications.

Tina stops behind a desk, removing her coat and hat. She
tries to regain her lost status in front of Newt by appearing

official, busying herself with papers.

> TINA
> So, you got your wand
> permit? All foreigners have to
> have them in New York.

> NEWT
> *(lying)*
> I made a postal application
> weeks ago.

> TINA
> *(now sitting on the desk,*
> *scribbles on a clipboard)*
> Scamander . . .
> *(finding him very fishy)*
> And you were just in
> Equatorial Guinea?

> NEWT
> I've just completed a year in
> the field. I'm writing a book
> about magical creatures.

> TINA
> Like—an extermination
> guide?

NEWT
No. A guide to help people
understand why we should
be protecting these creatures
instead of killing them.

ABERNATHY (O.S.)
GOLDSTEIN! Where is she?
Where is she? GOLDSTEIN!

Tina ducks behind her desk, which amuses Newt.

*Abernathy, a pompous jobsworth, enters. He immediately
realizes where Tina is hidden.*

ABERNATHY
Goldstein!

Tina, looking guilty, slowly emerges from behind the desk.

ABERNATHY
Did you just butt in on the
Investigative Team again?

Tina is about to defend herself, but Abernathy continues:

ABERNATHY
Where've you been?

TINA
(*awkward*)
What . . . ?

ABERNATHY
(*to Newt*)
Where'd she pick you up?

NEWT
Me?

Newt quickly looks at Tina, who shakes her head, her expression one of desperation. Newt stalls—a silent pact between him and Tina.

ABERNATHY
(*agitated with the lack
of information*)
Have you been tracking them
Second Salemers again?

TINA
Of course not, sir.

Graves comes around the corner. Abernathy is immediately cowed.

ABERNATHY
Afternoon, Mr. Graves, sir!

GRAVES
Afternoon, ah—Abernathy.

Tina steps forward to formally address Graves.

TINA
*(speaking quickly, eager to
have her case heard)*
Mr. Graves, sir, this is Mr.
Scamander—he has a crazy
creature in that case and it
got out and caused mayhem
in a bank, sir.

GRAVES
Let's see the little guy.

*Tina breathes a sigh of relief: Finally someone is listening
to her. Newt tries to speak up—he looks more panicky than
might seem warranted by a Niffler—but Graves dismisses
him.*

*Tina theatrically places the case onto a table and throws
open the lid. She looks aghast at the contents.*

*ANGLE ON THE CASE CONTENTS—it is full of
pastries.*

Newt approaches, nervous. On seeing the contents, he looks horrified. Graves looks confused, but smirks slightly— another one of Tina's mistakes.

> GRAVES
>
> Tina . . .

Graves walks away. Newt and Tina stare at each other.

SCENE 25
EXT. STREET ON THE LOWER EAST SIDE—DAY

Jacob marches along the overcast street, case in hand, past pushcarts, shabby little shops, and tenement buildings. He continually throws nervous glances over his shoulder.

SCENE 26
INT. JACOB'S ROOM—DAY

A tiny, dirty room, the furnishings sparse and shabby.

CLOSE ON THE CASE as Jacob throws it down onto his bed. He looks up at a portrait of his grandmother, which hangs on the wall.

> JACOB
> I'm sorry, Grandma.

Jacob sits down at his desk, hanging his head in his hands, downcast, tired. Behind him, one of the catches on the case flies open. Jacob turns . . .

He sits down on the bed and examines the case. The second catch now flicks open of its own accord, and the case begins to shake, emitting aggressive animalistic sounds. Jacob slowly backs away.

Tentatively, he leans forward . . . Suddenly the lid flies open and out bursts a Murtlap—a ratlike creature with an anemone-style growth on its back. Jacob grapples with it, holding it tightly in both hands as it struggles.

We whip back to the case, which flies open once again as an invisible being shoots out, crashing into the ceiling before smashing through the window.

The Murtlap lunges forward, biting Jacob on the neck, sending him crashing through furniture and tumbling to the floor.

The room shakes heavily, and the wall holding the picture of Jacob's grandma begins to crack before exploding, as more creatures escape off-screen.

SCENE 27
INT. SECOND SALEM CHURCH, MAIN HALL—MONTAGE—DAY

A dingy wooden church with darkened windows and a high mezzanine balcony. Modesty is playing a solitary variation of hopscotch, skipping in and out of a chalked grid.

> MODESTY
> My momma, your momma,
> gonna catch a witch,
> My momma, your momma,
> flying on a switch,
> My momma, your momma,
> witches never cry,
> My momma, your momma,
> witches gonna die!

As she sings we see the church is full of group paraphernalia—leaflets advertising Mary Lou's campaign, and a large version of the group's anti-witchcraft banner.

SCENE 28
INT. SECOND SALEM CHURCH—DAY

A pigeon coos from a high-up window. Credence steps forward, staring up toward it before mechanically clapping his hands. The pigeon flies away.

We follow Chastity as she moves through the church and opens the large double doors onto the street.

SCENE 29
EXT. SECOND SALEM CHURCH, BACKYARD—DAY

Chastity emerges from the church and rings a large dinner bell.

SCENE 30
INT. SECOND SALEM CHURCH, MAIN HALL—DAY

Modesty continues playing hopscotch. Credence pauses, looking past her and out toward the door.

> MODESTY
> . . . Witch number three,
>   gonna watch her burn,
> Witch number four, flogging
>   take a turn.

Young children stream into the church.

TIME CUT:

Brown soup is being ladled out to the children, who jostle

*each other to get near the front of the line. Mary Lou,
wearing an apron and looking on approvingly, squeezes
through the little crowd.*

> MARY LOU
> Collect your leaflets before
> you get food, children.

*Several of the children turn toward Chastity, who waits
primly, handing out campaign leaflets.*

TIME CUT:

*Mary Lou and Credence ladle out soup, Credence looking
intently into every face.*

*A boy with a birthmark on his face reaches the front of the
line. Credence stops his work and stares at him. Mary Lou
reaches out to touch the boy's face.*

> BOY
> Is it a witch's mark, ma'am?

> MARY LOU
> No. He's okay.

*The boy takes his soup and leaves. Credence stares after
him as they continue to serve.*

SCENE 31
EXT. BUSY STREET ON THE LOWER EAST SIDE—AFTERNOON

CLOSE ON A BILLYWIG—a small blue creature with helicopter-like wings on its head—flying high above the street.

Tina and Newt walk along the street, Tina carrying the case.

> TINA
> *(on the verge of tears)*
> I can't *believe* you didn't
> Obliviate that man! If there's
> an inquiry, I'm finished!

> NEWT
> So why would you be
> finished? I'm the one that's—

> TINA
> I'm not supposed to go near
> the Second Salemers!

The Billywig zooms over their heads. Newt spins, horrified, watching it.

TINA

What was that?

NEWT

Er—moth, I think. Big moth.

Tina finds this explanation dubious. They round a corner to find a crowd gathered in front of a crumbling building. People are shouting, others are hurriedly evacuating the building. A policeman is standing at the center of the crowd, being harassed by disgruntled tenement dwellers.

JUMP CUT TO:

Newt and Tina move around the outskirts of the crowd. At the back, a tipsy hobo is trying to attract the policeman's attention.

POLICEMAN

Hey . . . Hey—quiet
down—I'm trying to
get a statement . . .

HOUSEWIFE

. . . I'm telling you it's a gas
explosion again, I ain't taking
the kids back up there until
it's safe.

POLICEMAN
Sorry, ma'am—There ain't no
smell of gas.

HOBO
(*drunk*)
It warn't gas—hey,
Officer, I seen it!—it
wuzza—a gigantic—a huge
hippopotto—

*Tina is looking up at the ruined building, and misses Newt
sliding his wand from his sleeve and pointing it at the hobo.*

HOBO
—gas. It was gas.

The others in the crowd around him agree.

CROWD
Gas . . . It was gas!

*Tina again catches sight of the Billywig. Taking advantage
of this distraction, Newt runs up the metal steps and inside
the ruined tenement building.*

SCENE 32
INT. JACOB'S ROOM—AFTERNOON

Newt enters Jacob's room and stops, staring: The room is completely destroyed. Footprints, broken furniture, shattered glass. Even worse: a massive hole in the opposite wall—something huge has blasted its way out. We can hear Jacob groaning from the corner.

SCENE 33
EXT. TENEMENT STREET—AFTERNOON

CUT BACK TO TINA as she looks around and realizes that Newt has disappeared from the crowd.

SCENE 34
INT. JACOB'S ROOM—AFTERNOON

Newt crouches beside Jacob, who lies on his back, eyes closed and moaning. Newt tries to examine a small red bite

on Jacob's neck, but Jacob keeps unconsciously batting him away.

> TINA (O.S.)
> Mr. Scamander!

CUT TO TINA, running with purpose up the staircase of Jacob's building.

CUT BACK TO NEWT, who desperately performs a Repairing Charm. The room is righted, the wall repaired, just in time before Tina enters the room.

SCENE 35
INT. JACOB'S ROOM—AFTERNOON

Tina hurries inside to find Newt, trying to look innocent and composed, sitting on the bed. He calmly seals the latches on his case.

> TINA
> It was *open?*

> NEWT
> Just a smidge . . .

TINA
That crazy Niffler thing's on
the loose again?

NEWT
Er—it *might* be—

TINA
Then look for it! Look!

Jacob moans.

Tina drops Jacob's case and makes straight for the injured Jacob.

TINA
(*about Jacob, worried*)
His neck's bleeding, he's hurt!
Wake up, Mr. No-Maj . . .

With Tina's back turned, Newt makes toward the door. Suddenly Tina emits a guttural scream as the Murtlap comes scuttling out from under a cabinet and latches onto her arm. Newt spins, catching the creature by the tail and grappling it into the case.

TINA
Mercy Lewis, what is that?

NEWT
Nothing to worry about. That
is a Murtlap.

Unnoticed by either, Jacob opens his eyes.

TINA
What else have you got in
there?

JACOB
(recognizing Newt)
You!

NEWT
Hello.

TINA
Easy, Mr.—

JACOB
Kowalski . . . Jacob . . .

Tina takes Jacob's hand to shake it.

*Newt raises his wand. Jacob recoils in fear, clutching at
Tina, who moves protectively in front of him.*

TINA
You can't Obliviate him! We
need him as a witness.

NEWT
I'm sorry—you've just yelled
at me the length of New York
for not doing it in the first
place . . .

TINA
He's hurt! He looks ill!

NEWT
He'll be fine. Murtlap bites
aren't serious.

*Newt puts his wand away. Jacob retches into the corner,
while Tina looks at Newt in disbelief.*

NEWT
I admit that is a slightly more
severe reaction than I've seen,
but if it was really serious—
he'd have . . .

TINA
What?

NEWT
Well, the first symptom would
be flames out of his anus—

Terrified, Jacob feels the seat of his pants.

TINA
This is balled up!

NEWT
It'll last forty-eight hours at
most! I can keep him if you
want me to—

TINA
Oh, keep him? We don't
keep them! Mr. Scamander,
do you know *anything* about
the wizarding community in
America?

NEWT
I do know a few things,
actually. I know you have
rather backwards laws about
relations with non-magic
people. That you're not
meant to befriend them, that
you can't marry them, which
seems mildly absurd to me.

Jacob is following this conversation, openmouthed.

> TINA
> Who's going to marry him?
> You're both coming with
> me—

> NEWT
> I don't see why I need to
> come with you—

Tina tries to lift the only partly conscious Jacob from the floor.

> TINA
> Help me!

Newt feels obliged to help.

> JACOB
> I'm ... I'm dreaming, right?
> Yeah ... I'm tired, I never
> went to the bank. This is
> all just some big nightmare,
> right?

> TINA
> For the both of us, Mr.
> Kowalski.

Tina and Newt Disapparate with Jacob.

We focus on the photo of Jacob's grandma, once again hanging on the wall. Eventually the photo gives a little shake before falling and revealing a hole in the wall, inhabited by the Niffler.

SCENE 36
EXT. UPPER EAST SIDE—AFTERNOON

A young boy, clutching a huge lollipop, is led down the busy street by his father. As they pass a fruit barrow, an apple suddenly levitates, bobbing along beside him. The boy gazes in wonder as the apple is eaten by something invisible, then the smile fades as his lollipop is snatched by the same unseen hands.

At a newsstand, the eyes of a lady on an advertisement blink open. The outline of a creature becomes visible, camouflage-like, before it peels away from the poster. It

moves along the street, invisible again, only locatable by the lollipop it holds, seemingly suspended in midair. A dog barks in its direction, and the creature scuttles on, knocking over newspaper stands, causing bikes and cars to swerve.

ANGLE ON THE ROOF OF A DEPARTMENT STORE—we see a thin blue tail slither inside a small attic window. Suddenly the building shakes and tiles break away as the creature's size expands to fill the whole room.

SCENE 37
INT. SHAW TOWER NEWSROOM—DUSK

The glittering Art Deco headquarters of a media empire. Many journalists are hard at work in an outer office.

An elevator opens and Langdon Shaw bustles excitedly through the room, leading the Second Salemers. He carries maps, several old books, and a handful of photographs.

Mary Lou is composed, Chastity looks shy, and Modesty is excited, curious. Credence looks nervous—he doesn't like crowds.

LANGDON
. . . and so this is the newsroom.

Langdon spins around excitedly, eager to show the Second Salemers that he holds authority here.

LANGDON
Let's go!

Langdon moves around the office and speaks to some of the workers.

LANGDON
Hey, how are you? Make
way for the Barebones! Now,
they're just putting the papers
to bed, as they say.

Looks of veiled amusement from journalists as Langdon leads his group to double doors at the end of the open-plan area. Henry Shaw Sr.'s assistant—Barker—stands up, anxious.

BARKER
Mr. Shaw, sir, he's with the
senator—

LANGDON
Never mind that, Barker, I
wanna see my father!

Langdon pushes past.

SCENE 38
INT. SHAW SR.'S PENTHOUSE OFFICE—DUSK

A large, impressive office with spectacular views across the city. The newspaper magnate—Henry Shaw Sr.—is talking to his elder son, Senator Shaw.

> SENATOR SHAW
> . . . we could just buy the
> boats . . .

The doors burst open to reveal a harassed-looking Barker and an excitable Langdon.

> BARKER
> I'm so sorry, Mr. Shaw, but
> your son insisted—

> LANGDON
> Father, you're going to want
> to hear this.

Langdon moves toward his father's desk and begins spreading out photographs. We recognize some of the images: the destroyed streets from the start of the film.

LANGDON
I've got something huge!

SHAW SR.
Your brother and I are busy
here, Langdon. Working on
his campaign. We don't have
time for this.

*Mary Lou, Credence, Chastity, and Modesty enter the
office. Shaw Sr. and Senator Shaw stare. Credence stands
with his head bowed, embarrassed, nervous.*

LANGDON
This is Mary Lou Barebone
from the New Salem
Philanthropic Society, and
she's got a big story for you!

SHAW SR.
Oh, she has, has she?

LANGDON
There's strange things going
on all over the city. The
people behind this—they are
not like you and me. This is
witchcraft, don't you see.

*Shaw Sr. and the senator look dubious—all too used to
Langdon's harebrained little projects and interests.*

SHAW SR.
Langdon.

LANGDON
She doesn't want any money.

SHAW SR.
Then either her story is
worthless, or she's lying about
the cost. Nobody gives away
anything valuable for free.

MARY LOU
(confident, persuasive)
You are right, Mr. Shaw.
What we desire is infinitely
more valuable than money:
It's your influence. Millions
of people read your
newspapers and they need
to be made aware about this
danger.

LANGDON
The crazy disturbances in
the subway—just look at the
pictures!

SHAW SR.
I'd like you and your friends
to leave.

LANGDON
No, you're missing a
trick here. Just look at the
evidence—

SHAW SR.
Really.

SENATOR SHAW
*(joining his father and
brother)*
Langdon. Just listen to Father
and go.

His eyes shift, focus on Credence.

SENATOR SHAW
And take the freaks with you.

*Credence perceptibly twitches, disturbed by anger in his
vicinity. Mary Lou is calm but steely.*

LANGDON
This is Father's office, not
yours, and I'm sick of this
every time I walk in here . . .

*Shaw Sr. silences his son and motions for the Barebones to
leave.*

SHAW SR.
That's it—thank you.

MARY LOU
(calm, dignified)
We hope you'll reconsider,
Mr. Shaw. We're not difficult
to find. Until then, we thank
you for your time.

*Shaw Sr. and Senator Shaw watch Mary Lou as she turns,
leading her children out. The newsroom has fallen quiet,
everyone craning to hear the row.*

*As he departs, Credence drops a leaflet. Senator Shaw
moves forward and bends to pick it up. He glances at the
witches on the front.*

SENATOR SHAW
(to Credence)
Hey, boy. You dropped
something.

*The senator crumples up the leaflet before putting it in
Credence's hand.*

SENATOR SHAW
Here you go, freak—why
don't you put that in the trash
where you all belong.

*Behind Credence, Modesty's eyes burn. She clutches
Credence's hand protectively.*

SCENE 39
EXT. BROWNSTONE STREET—SHORTLY
AFTERWARD—DUSK

*Tina and Newt stand on either side of an ailing Jacob,
trying to keep him steady.*

> TINA
> Take a right here . . .

*Jacob makes various retching sounds, the bite on his neck
clearly affecting him more and more.*

*As the group rounds a corner, Tina hurries them to hide
behind a large repair truck. From here she peers at a house
across the street.*

> TINA
> Okay—before we go in—I'm
> not supposed to have men on
> the premises.

> NEWT
> In that case, Mr. Kowalski
> and I can easily seek other
> accommodation—

> TINA
> Oh no, you don't!

Tina quickly grabs Jacob's arm and pulls him across the road, Newt dutifully following.

> TINA
> Watch your step.

SCENE 40
INT. GOLDSTEIN RESIDENCE, STAIRWELL— DUSK

Newt, Tina, and Jacob tiptoe up the stairs. They have just reached the first landing when Mrs. Esposito, the landlady, calls out. The group freezes.

> MRS. ESPOSITO (O.S.)
> That you, Tina?

TINA
Yes, Mrs. Esposito!

MRS. ESPOSITO (O.S.)
Are you alone?

TINA
I'm always alone, Mrs.
Esposito!

A beat.

SCENE 41
INT. GOLDSTEIN RESIDENCE, SITTING ROOM—DUSK

The group enters the Goldstein apartment.

Although impoverished, the apartment is enlivened by workaday magic. An iron is working away on its own in a corner, and a clotheshorse revolves clumsily on its wooden legs in front of the fire, drying an assortment of underwear. Magazines are scattered around: The Witch's Friend, Witch Chat, *and* Transfiguration Today.

*Blond Queenie, the most beautiful girl ever to don witches'
robes, is standing in a silk slip, supervising the mending of
a dress on a dressmaker's dummy. Jacob is thunderstruck.*

*Newt barely notices. Impatient to leave as soon as possible,
he starts peeking out the windows.*

> QUEENIE
> Teenie—you brought men
> home?

> TINA
> Gentlemen, this is my sister.
> You want to put something
> on, Queenie?

> QUEENIE
> *(unconcerned)*
> Oh, sure—

*She runs her wand up the dummy and the dress runs
magically up her body. Jacob watches the display,
dumbfounded.*

Tina, frustrated, starts tidying the apartment.

> QUEENIE
> So, who are they?

TINA
That's Mr. Scamander.
He's committed a serious
infraction of the National
Statute of Secrecy—

QUEENIE
(impressed)
He's a *criminal*?

TINA
—uh-huh, and this is Mr.
Kowalski, he's a No-Maj—

QUEENIE
(suddenly worried)
A No-Maj? Teen—what are
you up to?

TINA
He's sick—it's a long story—
Mr. Scamander has lost
something, I'm going to help
him find it.

Jacob suddenly staggers, very sweaty and unwell. Queenie runs to him as Tina hovers, also worried.

QUEENIE
(as Jacob falls back onto a sofa)
You need to sit down, honey.

Hey—
> (*reading his mind*)

—he hasn't eaten all day.
And—
> (*reading his mind*)

—aw, that's rough,
> (*reading his mind*)

—he didn't get the money he
wanted for his bakery. You
bake, honey? I love to cook.

*Newt is watching Queenie from his spot by the window, his
scientific attention now aroused.*

NEWT
You're a Legilimens?

QUEENIE
Uh-huh, yeah. But I always
have trouble with your kind.
Brits. It's the accent.

JACOB
(*cottoning on, appalled*)
You know how to read minds?

QUEENIE
Aw, don't worry, honey. Most
guys think what you was
thinking, first time they see me.

Queenie playfully gestures toward Jacob with her wand.

QUEENIE
Now, you need food.

Newt looks out the window and sees a Billywig fly past—he's nervous, impatient to get out and find his creatures.

Tina and Queenie busy themselves in the kitchen. Ingredients come floating out of cupboards as Queenie enchants them into the components of a meal—carrots and apples chop themselves, pastry rolls itself, and pans stir.

QUEENIE
(to Tina)
Hot dog . . . again?

TINA
Don't read my mind!

QUEENIE
Not a very wholesome lunch.

Tina points her wand at the cupboards. Dishes, assorted cutlery, and glasses come flying out, setting themselves on the table with a little prodding from Tina's wand. Jacob, half-fascinated, half-terrified, staggers toward the table.

ANGLE ON NEWT, his hand on the doorknob.

>QUEENIE
>*(artless)*
>Hey, Mr. Scamander, you
>prefer pie or strudel?

All look at Newt, who, embarrassed, removes his hand from the doorknob.

>NEWT
>I really don't have a
>preference.

Tina stares at Newt: confrontational, but also disappointed and hurt.

Jacob is already seated at the table, tucking his napkin into his shirt.

>QUEENIE
>*(reading Jacob's mind)*
>You prefer strudel, huh,
>honey? Strudel it is.

Jacob nods with excited enthusiasm. Queenie grins back, delighted.

With a flick of her wand, Queenie sends raisins, apples, and pastry flying into the air. The concoction neatly wraps itself up into a cylindrical pie, baking on the spot, complete with ornate decoration and a dusting of sugar. Jacob takes a deep breath in: heaven.

Tina lights candles on the table—the meal is ready.

*FOCUS ON NEWT'S POCKET—a small squeak, and
Pickett pokes his head out, curious.*

> TINA
> Well, sit down, Mr.
> Scamander, we're not going
> to poison you.

*Newt, still hovering near the door, looks somewhat charmed
by the situation. Jacob glares at him subtly, willing him to
sit down.*

SCENE 42
EXT. BROADWAY—NIGHT

Credence is walking alone through a worldly crowd of late-night diners and theatergoers. Traffic roars past. He is trying to give out leaflets but is met with only incredulity and faint derision.

The Woolworth Building looms ahead. Credence glances toward it with a hint of longing. Graves stands outside, watching Credence intently. Credence spots him, hope flickering across his face. Utterly enthralled, Credence moves across the street toward Graves, barely looking where he's going—everything else is forgotten.

SCENE 43
EXT. ALLEYWAY—NIGHT

Credence stands, head bowed, at the end of a dimly lit alleyway. Graves joins him, moving in very close to whisper, conspiratorial:

> GRAVES
> You're upset. It's your mother again. Somebody's said something—what did they say? Tell me.

> CREDENCE
> Do you think I'm a freak?

> GRAVES
> No—I think you're a very special young man or I wouldn't have asked you to help me, now would I?

A pause. Graves rests a hand on Credence's arm. The human contact seems to both startle and captivate Credence.

GRAVES
Have you any news?

CREDENCE
I'm still looking. Mr. Graves,
if I knew whether it was a girl
or boy—

GRAVES
My vision showed only the
child's immense power. He
or she is no older than ten,
and I saw this child in close
proximity to your mother—
she I saw so plainly.

CREDENCE
That could be any one of
hundreds.

Graves's tone softens—he's beguiling, comforting.

GRAVES
There is something else.
Something I haven't told you.
I saw you beside me in New

York. You're the one that
gains this child's trust. You
are the key—I saw this. You
want to join the wizarding
world. I want those things
too, Credence. I want them
for you. So find the child.
Find the child and we'll all be
free.

SCENE 44
INT. GOLDSTEIN RESIDENCE, SITTING
ROOM—HALF HOUR LATER—NIGHT

The catch on Newt's case pops open. Newt reaches down and pushes it shut.

Jacob looks a little better for having eaten. He and Queenie are getting on famously.

> QUEENIE
> The job ain't that glamorous.
> I mean, I spend most days
> making coffee, unjinxing the
> john . . . Tina's the career girl.

(she reads his mind)
Nah. We're orphans. Ma and
Pa died of dragon pox when
we were kids. Aw . . .
(reading his mind)
You're sweet. But we got each
other!

JACOB
Could you stop reading my
mind for a second? Don't get
me wrong—I love it.

Queenie giggles, delighted, captivated by Jacob.

JACOB
This meal—it's insanely good!
This is what I do—I'm a cook
and this is, like, the greatest
meal I have ever had in my
life.

QUEENIE
(laughing)
Oh, you slay me! I ain't never
really talked to a No-Maj
before.

JACOB
Really?

Queenie and Jacob gaze into each other's eyes. Newt and Tina sit opposite each other, uncomfortably silent in the presence of such affectionate behavior.

> QUEENIE
> *(to Tina)*
> I am not flirting!

> TINA
> *(embarrassed)*
> I'm just saying—don't go
> getting attached, he's going to
> have to be Obliviated!
> *(to Jacob)*
> It's nothing personal.

Jacob is suddenly very pale and sweaty again, although still trying to look good for Queenie.

> QUEENIE
> *(to Jacob)*
> Oh, hey, you okay, honey?

Newt briskly gets up from the table and awkwardly stands behind his chair.

> NEWT
> Miss Goldstein, I think Mr.
> Kowalski could do with an
> early night. And besides, you

and I will need to be up early
tomorrow morning to find
my Niffler, so—

QUEENIE
(to Tina)
What's a Niffler?

Tina looks put out.

TINA
Don't ask.
(moving toward a back room)
Okay, you guys can bunk in
here.

SCENE 45
INT. GOLDSTEIN RESIDENCE, BEDROOM—
NIGHT

The boys are tucked up in neatly made twin beds. Newt is
resolutely turned away on his side, while Jacob is sitting up,
trying to make sense of a wizarding book.

Tina, wearing patterned blue pajamas, tentatively knocks

*on the door, and enters carrying a tray of cocoa. The mugs
are stirring themselves—Jacob is captivated again.*

> TINA
> I thought you might like a hot
> drink?

*Tina carefully hands Jacob his mug. Newt remains turned
away, feigning sleep, so Tina, with some frustration,
pointedly places his cup on the bedside table.*

> JACOB
> Hey, Mr. Scamander—
> *(to Newt, trying to make
> him friendlier)*
> Look, cocoa!

Newt does not move.

> TINA
> *(irritated)*
> The toilet's down the hall to
> the right.

> JACOB
> Thanks . . .

*As Tina shuts the door, Jacob gets a quick glimpse of Queenie in
the other room, wearing a much less demure dressing gown.*

JACOB
Very much . . .

The moment the door closes Newt jumps up, still wearing his overcoat, and places his case on the floor. To Jacob's utter astonishment, Newt opens the case and walks down inside it, now completely out of sight.

Jacob lets out a small scream of alarm.

Newt's hand appears from the case, beckoning him imperiously. Jacob stares, breathing heavily, trying to process the situation.

Newt's hand, impatient, appears again.

NEWT (O.S.)
Come on.

Jacob rallies himself, gets out of bed, and steps down into Newt's case. However, he gets stuck at his waistline and tries hard to squeeze himself through, the case bouncing up and down with his efforts.

JACOB
For the love of . . .

With a final frustrated jump, Jacob suddenly disappears through the case, which snaps shut after him.

SCENE 46
INT. NEWT'S CASE—A MOMENT LATER—
NIGHT

Jacob crashes down the steps of the case, colliding with various objects, instruments, and bottles as he goes.

He finds himself inside a small wooden shed containing a camp bed, tropical gear, and various tools hung up on the walls. Wooden cupboards contain rope, nets, and collecting jars. A very old typewriter, a pile of manuscripts, and a medieval bestiary sit on a desk. Potted plants line a shelf. Rows of pills and tablets, syringes and vials form a

medicine chest, and tacked up on the walls are notes, maps, drawings, and a few moving photographs of extraordinary creatures. A dried carcass hangs from a hook. Several sacks of feed are resting against the wall.

NEWT
(glances at Jacob)
Will you sit down.

Jacob drops onto a crate hand labeled: MOONCALF PELLETS.

JACOB
That's good.

Newt moves forward to examine the bite on Jacob's neck—one quick glance:

NEWT
Ah, that's definitely the
Murtlap. You must be
particularly susceptible.
See, you're a Muggle. So
our physiologies are subtly
different.

Newt busies himself at his workstation, using plants and the contents of various bottles to create a poultice, which he rapidly applies to Jacob's neck.

JACOB
Ow . . .

NEWT
Now stay still. Now that
should stop the sweating.
(handing him some pills)
And one of those should sort
the twitch.

Jacob looks suspiciously at the pills in his hand. Finally, deciding he has nothing to lose, he swallows them.

ANGLE ON NEWT, who has now removed his waistcoat, undone his bow tie, and lowered his braces. He picks up a meat cleaver and hacks chunks of meat off a large carcass before tossing them into a bucket.

NEWT
(handing him the bucket)
Take that.

Jacob looks disgusted. Newt doesn't notice, his attention now focused on a spiny cocoon, which he slowly begins to squeeze. As he does so, the cocoon emits a luminous venom, which Newt collects into a glass vial.

NEWT
(to the cocoon)
Come on . . .

JACOB
What you got there?

NEWT
Well, this—the locals call
"Swooping Evil"—not the
friendliest of names. It's quite
an agile fellow.

As if to demonstrate, Newt flicks the cocoon, which unravels, dangling elegantly from his finger.

NEWT
I've been studying him.
And I am pretty sure his
venom could be quite useful
if properly diluted. Just to
remove bad memories, you
know.

Quite suddenly Newt throws the Swooping Evil toward Jacob. The creature bursts out from its cocoon—a batlike, spiky, colorful creature—and howls in Jacob's face before Newt recalls it. Jacob recoils dramatically, but this was evidently Newt's idea of a little joke . . .

NEWT
(smiling to himself)
Probably shouldn't let him
loose in here, though.

Newt opens the door of his shed and walks through.

> NEWT

Come on.

Jacob, now thoroughly startled, follows him out.

SCENE 47
INT. NEWT'S CASE, ANIMAL AREA—DAY

The perimeter of the leather case is dimly visible, but the place has swollen to the size of a small aircraft hangar. It contains what appears to be a safari park in miniature. Each of Newt's creatures has its own perfect, magically realized habitat.

Jacob steps into this world, totally amazed.

Newt is standing in the nearest habitat—a slice of Arizona desert. This area contains a magnificent Thunderbird—a creature like a large albatross, its glorious wings shimmering with cloud- and sunlike patterns. One of its legs is rubbed raw and bloody—it has obviously been chained previously.

As the Thunderbird flaps its wings, its habitat fills with a torrential downpour, thunder, and lightning. Newt uses his

wand to create a magical umbrella, shielding him from the rain.

> NEWT
> *(eyes on the Thunderbird up high)*
> Come on—come on . . . Down
> you come . . . Come on.

Slowly the Thunderbird calms itself, lowering down to stand on a large rock in front of Newt. As it does, the rain dies down and is replaced by a brilliant, hot sunshine.

Newt puts his wand away and produces a handful of grubs from his pocket. The Thunderbird watches intently.

Newt strokes the Thunderbird with his free hand, calming him, affectionate.

> NEWT
> Oh, thank Paracelsus. If you'd
> have got out that could have
> been quite catastrophic.
> *(to Jacob)*
> You see, he's the real reason
> I came to America. To bring
> Frank home.

Jacob, still staring, steps slowly forward. In reaction, the Thunderbird starts to flap his wings, agitated.

NEWT
(to Jacob)
No, sorry—stay there—he's a
wee bit sensitive to strangers.
(to the Thunderbird, calming)
Here you are—here you are.
(to Jacob)
He was trafficked, you see. I
found him in Egypt, he was
all chained up. Couldn't leave
him there, had to bring him
back. I'm going to put you
back where you belong, aren't
I, Frank. To the wilds of
Arizona.

Newt, his face full of hope and expectation, hugs Frank's head. Then, grinning, he casts the handful of grubs high into the air. Frank soars majestically upward after them, sunlight bursting from his wings.

Newt watches him fly with love and pride. Then he turns, puts his hands to his mouth, and roars, beast-like, toward another area of the case.

Newt moves past Jacob, grabbing the bucket of meat.

Jacob stumbles after him as several Doxys buzz around his head. Dazed, he swats them out of the way. Behind him a large dung beetle rolls a giant ball of dung.

We hear Newt roar loudly again. Jacob hurries toward the sound, finding Newt in a sandy, moonlit territory.

NEWT
(under his breath)
Ah—here they come.

JACOB
Here who comes?

NEWT
The Graphorns.

A large creature comes charging into sight: a Graphorn— built like a saber-toothed tiger but with slimy tentacles at its mouth. Jacob screams and tries to back off, but Newt grabs hold of his arm, stopping him.

NEWT
You're all right. You're all
right.

The Graphorn moves closer to Newt.

NEWT
(stroking the Graphorn)
Hello, hello!

The Graphorn's strange slimy tentacles rest on Newt's shoulder, seeming to embrace him.

NEWT

So they're the last breeding
pair in existence. If I hadn't
managed to rescue them, that
could have been the end of
Graphorns—forever.

*A younger Graphorn trots straight up to Jacob and begins
licking his hand, circling him curiously. He stares down
at it, then gently reaches out and strokes its head. Newt
watches Jacob, pleased.*

NEWT

All right.

*Newt throws a piece of meat into the enclosure, which is
hastily chased and consumed by the young Graphorn.*

JACOB

So what, you—you rescue
these creatures?

NEWT

Yes, that's right. Rescue,
nurture, and protect them, and
I'm gently trying to educate my
fellow wizards about them.

*A tiny bright pink bird, the Fwooper, flies past and comes to
rest on a little perch, suspended from midair.*

Newt heads up a small ramp of stairs.

> NEWT
> *(to Jacob)*
> Come on.

They enter a bamboo wood, ducking and diving through the trees. Newt calls out:

> NEWT
> Titus? Finn? Poppy, Marlow,
> Tom?

They emerge into a sunlit glade, Newt producing Pickett from his pocket and holding him perched on his hand.

> NEWT
> *(to Jacob)*
> He had a cold. He needed
> some body warmth.

> JACOB
> Aw.

They move toward a small tree bathed in sunlight. At their approach, a clan of Bowtruckles chatters and rushes out of the leaves.

Newt extends his arm toward the tree, trying to persuade Pickett to rejoin the others. The Bowtruckles clack noisily when they see Pickett.

NEWT
Right, on you hop.

Pickett steadfastly refuses to leave Newt's arm.

NEWT
(to Jacob)
See, he has some attachment
issues.
(to Pickett)
Now, come on, Pickett.
Pickett. No, they're not going
to bully you . . . Now, come
on. Pickett!

*Pickett clings by his spindly hands to one of Newt's fingers,
desperate not to return to the tree. Newt finally resigns
himself.*

NEWT
All right. But that is exactly
why they accuse me of
favoritism . . .

*Newt puts Pickett onto his shoulder and turns. On seeing a
large, round, empty nest, he looks concerned.*

NEWT
(devastated)
I wonder where Dougal's
gone.

From within a nearby nest, we hear chirping sounds.

> NEWT
> All right, I'm coming . . . I'm
> coming, Mum's here—Mum's
> here.

Newt reaches into the nest and scoops up a baby Occamy.

> NEWT
> Ah—hello, you—let me take a
> look at you.

> JACOB
> I know these guys.

> NEWT
> New Occamy.
> *(to Jacob)*
> Your Occamy.

> JACOB
> What do you mean? My
> Occamy?

> NEWT
> Yes—do you want to . . . ?

Newt proffers the Occamy to Jacob.

> JACOB
> Oh wow . . . Yeah, sure.
> Okay . . . Ah-ha.

Jacob holds the newborn creature gently in his hands and stares. As he moves to stroke its head, the Occamy moves to nip him. Jacob starts backward.

> NEWT
> Ah no, sorry—don't pet
> them. They learn to defend
> themselves early. See, their
> shells are made of silver so
> they're incredibly valuable.

Newt feeds the other babies in the nest.

> JACOB
> Okay . . .

> NEWT
> Their nests tend to get
> ransacked by hunters.

Newt, delighted by Jacob's interest in his creatures, takes back the baby Occamy, placing it in the nest.

> JACOB
> Thank you.
> (croaky)
> Mr. Scamander?

NEWT
Call me Newt.

JACOB
Newt . . . I don't think I'm
dreaming.

NEWT
(vaguely amused)
What gave it away?

JACOB
I ain't got the brains to make
this up.

Newt looks at Jacob, both intrigued and flattered.

NEWT
Actually, would you
mind throwing some of
those pellets in with the
Mooncalves over there?

JACOB
Yeah, sure.

Jacob bends down and picks up the bucket of pellets.

NEWT
Just over there . . .

Newt grabs a nearby wheelbarrow and sets off farther into the case.

> NEWT
> *(annoyed)*
> Bugger—Niffler's gone. Of
> course he has, little bugger.
> Any chance to get his hands
> on something shiny.

As Jacob walks through the case, we see what appear to be golden "leaves" falling from a tiny tree, which move together en masse toward the camera. They swarm upward, mingling with Doxys, Glow Bugs, and Grindylows, which float through the air.

The camera pans up to reveal another magnificent creature, the Nundu—looking almost exactly like a lion, it has a large mane that bursts forth when it roars. It stands proudly on a large rock, roaring at the moon. Newt scatters food at its feet and purposefully moves on.

A Diricawl—a small, plump bird—waddles in the foreground, followed by its constantly Apparating chicks, as Jacob climbs up a steep grassy bank.

> JACOB
> *(to himself)*
> What did you do today,
> Jacob? I was inside a suitcase.

At the top, Jacob finds a large moonlit rock face populated by little Mooncalves—shy, with huge eyes filling their whole faces.

JACOB
Hey! Oh, hello, fellas—all
right—all right.

The Mooncalves jump and hop down the rocks toward Jacob, who finds himself suddenly surrounded by their friendly, hopeful faces.

JACOB
Take it easy—take it easy.

As he throws pellets, the Mooncalves bob eagerly up and down. Jacob visibly seems to be feeling better—he really likes this . . .

ANGLE ON NEWT, now cradling a luminescent creature with sprouting alien-like tendrils. He feeds the creature with a bottle, while carefully watching how Jacob handles the Mooncalves—he recognizes a kindred spirit.

JACOB
(still feeding the
Mooncalves)
There you go, cutie. Ah, there
it is.

A kind of icy cry echoes from nearby.

> JACOB
> *(toward Newt)*
> Did you hear that?

But Newt is gone. Jacob turns to see a curtain billowing open, behind which is revealed a snowscape.

We push inward, toward a small, oleaginous black mass suspended in midair—an Obscurus. Jacob, intrigued, moves into the snowscape to get a closer look.

The mass continues to swirl, emitting a disturbed, restless energy. Jacob reaches out to touch it.

> NEWT (O.S.)
> *(sharp)*
> Step back.

Jacob jumps.

> JACOB
> Jeez . . .

> NEWT
> Step back . . .

> JACOB
> What's the matter with this?

> NEWT
> I said step away.

> JACOB
> What the hell is this thing?

> NEWT
> It's an Obscurus.

Jacob looks at Newt, who is momentarily lost in a bad reverie. Newt turns abruptly away and heads back toward the hut, his tone colder, more efficient, no longer happy to play about in the case.

> NEWT
> I need to get going, find
> everyone who's escaped
> before they get hurt.

The pair enters another forest, Newt plowing ahead, on a mission.

> JACOB
> Before *they* could get hurt.

> NEWT
> Yes, Mr. Kowalski. See,
> they're currently in alien
> terrain, surrounded by
> millions of the most vicious
> creatures on the planet.

A beat.

> NEWT
>
> Humans.

Newt stops once more, staring into a large savannah enclosure, which is empty of any beasts.

> NEWT
>
> So where would you say that
> a medium-sized creature that
> likes broad, open plains—
> trees—water holes—that kind
> of thing—where might she go?

> JACOB
>
> In New York City?

> NEWT
>
> Yes.

> JACOB
>
> Plains?

Jacob shrugs as he tries to think of somewhere.

> JACOB
>
> Ah—Central Park?

NEWT
And where is that exactly?

JACOB
Where is Central Park?

A beat.

JACOB
Well, look, I would come and
show you, but don't you think
it's kind of a double cross?
The girls take us in—they
make us hot cocoa . . .

NEWT
You do realize that when they
see you've stopped sweating,
they'll Obliviate you in a
heartbeat.

JACOB
What does "Bliviate" mean?

NEWT
It'll be like you wake up and
all memory of magic is gone.

JACOB
I won't remember any of this?

He looks around. This world is extraordinary.

> NEWT

No.

> JACOB

All right, yeah—okay—I'll
help you.

> NEWT
> *(picking up a bucket)*

Come on, then.

SCENE 48
EXT./INT. STREET OUTSIDE THE SECOND SALEM CHURCH—NIGHT

Credence walks home toward the church. He looks happier than before: His meeting with Graves comforted him.

Credence slowly enters the church, shutting the double doors quietly.

Chastity is in the kitchen area—drying crockery.

Mary Lou sits in semidarkness on the stairs. Credence

senses her and pauses, his face one of trepidation.

> MARY LOU
> Credence—where have you
> been?

> CREDENCE
> I was . . . looking for a place
> for tomorrow's meeting.
> There's a corner on Thirty-
> Second that could—

Credence moves around to the bottom of the stairs, falling silent at the severe expression on Mary Lou's face.

> CREDENCE
> I'm sorry, Ma. I didn't realize
> it was so late.

As if on autopilot, Credence removes his belt. Mary Lou stands and extends her hand, taking the belt. In silence, she turns and walks up the stairs—Credence obediently following.

Modesty moves to the bottom of the stairs, watching them go, a look of fear and upset on her face.

SCENE 49
EXT. CENTRAL PARK—NIGHT

*A large frozen pond in the middle of Central Park.
Children ice-skate. A boy takes a tumble. A girl comes to
help him up, they link hands.*

*As they are about to stand, a light becomes visible
underneath the ice. A deep rumbling sound echoes. The
children stare as a glowing beast glides under the ice
beneath them, and off into the distance.*

SCENE 50
EXT. DIAMOND DISTRICT—NIGHT

*Newt and Jacob walk along another deserted street on
the way to Central Park. The shops around them are full
of expensive jewelry, diamonds, precious stones. Newt,
carrying his case, scans the shadows for small movements.*

NEWT
I was watching you at dinner.

JACOB
Yeah.

NEWT
People like you, don't they,
Mr. Kowalski?

JACOB
(startled)
Oh—well, I'm—I'm sure
people like you too—huh?

NEWT
(not very concerned)
No, not really. I annoy
people.

JACOB
(not sure how to answer)
Ahh.

Newt seems thoroughly intrigued by Jacob.

NEWT
Why did you decide to be a
baker?

JACOB
Ah well, um—because I'm
dying—in that canning
factory.
(off Newt's look)
Everyone there's dying. It

just crushes the life outta you.
You like canned food?

> NEWT

No.

> JACOB

Me neither. That's why I
want to make pastries, you
know. It makes people happy.
We're going this way.

Jacob heads off to his right. Newt follows.

> NEWT

So did you get your loan?

> JACOB

Er, no—I ain't got no
collateral. Stayed in the army
too long, apparently—I don't
know.

> NEWT

What, you fought in the war?

> JACOB

Of course I fought in the war,
everyone fought in the war—
you didn't fight in the war?

NEWT
I worked mostly with
dragons, Ukrainian
Ironbellies—Eastern Front.

*Newt suddenly stops. He has noticed a small shiny earring
lying on top of a car bonnet. His eyes move downward:
Diamonds are scattered across the pavement leading
toward the window of one particular diamond shop.*

*Newt stealthily follows the trail, creeping past shop
windows. Something catches his eye and suddenly, he
pauses. Very slowly, he tiptoes backward.*

*The Niffler is standing in a shop window. In order to hide,
it is emulating a jewelry stand, little arms outstretched,
covered in diamonds.*

*Newt stares at the Niffler in disbelief. Sensing Newt's stare,
the Niffler slowly turns. The two of them make eye contact.*

A beat.

*Suddenly the Niffler is off: scurrying farther into the shop
and away from Newt. Newt whips out his wand:*

NEWT
Finestra.

The window glass shatters and Newt leaps inside, seizing at

drawers and cupboards, desperate to find the creature.
Jacob stares down the street, incredulous as he watches
Newt, who, from an outsider's perspective, appears to be
looting the diamond shop.

The Niffler appears, scurrying over Newt's shoulders
in an attempt to get higher and away from his clutches.
Newt jumps onto a desk after him, but the Niffler is now
balancing on a crystal chandelier.

Newt reaches out and trips, both he and the Niffler now
hanging from the chandelier as it swings wildly round and
round.

Jacob looks around the street nervously, checking if anyone
else can hear the chaos coming from within the shop.

Finally the chandelier crashes to the floor, smashing.
Straight away the Niffler is back up, clambering across
cases full of jewelry, Newt in hot pursuit.

A catch opens on Newt's case, and a roar comes from
within. Jacob fearfully looks toward the case.

The Niffler and Newt continue their chase, finally
climbing onto a jewelry case that can't take their weight.
The case, with them both on top, falls to rest against one of
the shop windows. Both Newt and the Niffler become very
still . . .

Jacob breathes deeply and slowly moves forward to close the latch on the case.

Suddenly a crack appears on the window. Newt watches as the crack spreads across the pane of glass and the window bursts open, shattering across the pavement—Newt and the Niffler crashing to the ground.

The Niffler is still only for a moment before running off down the street. Newt quickly gathers himself, drawing his wand:

NEWT

ACCIO!

In slow motion the Niffler sails backward through the air toward Newt. As he flies, he looks sideways at the most glorious window display yet. His eyes widen. Jewelry falls from his pouch, flying toward Newt and Jacob, who duck and dive as they run forward toward the creature.

Passing a lamppost, the Niffler stretches out an arm, spinning around the pole and flying onward, out of the trajectory Newt had him on, and toward the glorious window.

Newt casts a spell toward the window, turning it into a sticky jelly, which finally traps the Niffler.

NEWT
(to the Niffler)
All right? Happy?

Newt, now covered in jewelry, pulls the Niffler from the window.

We hear police sirens in the background.

NEWT
One down—two to go.

Police cars come racing through the streets.

Newt once again sets about shaking all the diamonds from the Niffler's pocket.

The police cars pull up, and policemen run out, guns aimed at Newt and Jacob. Jacob, also covered in jewels, holds up his hands in surrender.

JACOB
They went that way,
Officer . . .

POLICE OFFICER 1
Hands up!

The Niffler, stuffed into Newt's overcoat, pokes out its little nose and squeaks.

POLICE OFFICER 2
What the hell is THAT?

Jacob suddenly looks to the left, his face one of terror.

> JACOB
> *(barely able to speak)*
> Lion . . .

A beat and then, in unison, the police turn both their eyes and their guns toward the other end of the street.

Perplexed, Newt looks too . . . A lion is stalking toward them.

> NEWT
> *(calm)*
> You know, New York is
> considerably more interesting
> than I'd expected.

Before the police can look back, Newt grabs Jacob and they Disapparate.

<u>SCENE 51</u>
EXT. CENTRAL PARK—NIGHT

Newt and Jacob hurry through the frost-covered park.

As they cross a bridge, they are almost bowled over by an ostrich, which tears past them—running for its life.

A loud rumble can be heard in the distance.

Newt tugs protective headgear out of his pocket and hands it to Jacob.

> NEWT
> Put this on.

> JACOB
> Why—why would I have to
> wear something like this?

> NEWT
> Because your skull is
> susceptible to breakage under
> immense force.

Newt runs on. Utterly terrified, Jacob puts on the hat and chases after Newt.

SCENE 52
EXT. GOLDSTEIN RESIDENCE—NIGHT

Tina and Queenie lean out of their bedroom window, craning into the dark. Another bellowing roar reverberates through the winter night. Other windows open, neighbors stare sleepily over the city.

SCENE 53
INT. GOLDSTEIN RESIDENCE—NIGHT

Tina and Queenie burst into the bedroom where Jacob and Newt are meant to be asleep. Every trace of the two men has gone. Furious, Tina storms off to dress. Queenie looks upset.

> QUEENIE
> But we made 'em cocoa . . .

SCENE 54
EXT. CENTRAL PARK ZOO—NIGHT

Newt and Jacob run up to the now half-empty zoo, the outer walls of which have been demolished in places. A large pile of rubble lies at the entrance.

Another bellowing roar echoes around the brick building. Newt produces a body protector.

> NEWT
> Okay, if you just, uh, pop this on.

Newt stands behind Jacob, fastening the breastplate over him.

> JACOB
> Okay.

> NEWT
> Now, there's absolutely
> nothing for you to worry
> about.

> JACOB
> Tell me—has anyone ever
> believed you when you told
> them not to worry?

> NEWT
> My philosophy is that worry-
> ing means you suffer twice.

Jacob digests Newt's "wisdom."

Newt picks up his case and Jacob follows him, stumbling over rubble and debris.

They stand at the entrance to the zoo. A loud snort comes from within.

> NEWT
> She's in season. She needs to
> mate.

ANGLE ON THE ERUMPENT—*a large, rotund, rhino-like creature with a massive horn protruding from her forehead. Five times his size, she is nuzzling up against the enclosure of a terrified hippo.*

Newt takes out a tiny vial of liquid—he pulls the stopper out with his teeth and spits it to the side before dabbing a spot of the liquid onto each wrist. Jacob looks at him—the smell is pungent.

> NEWT
> Erumpent musk—she is mad
> for it.

Newt passes Jacob the open bottle and heads into the zoo.

TIME CUT:

Newt places his case down on the ground near the Erumpent and slowly, seductively, opens it.

He begins to perform a "mating ritual"—a series of grunts, wiggles, rolls, and groans—to gain the Erumpent's attention.

Finally the Erumpent turns away from the hippo—she is interested in Newt. They face each other, circle round, undulating weirdly. The Erumpent's demeanor is puppy-like, her horn glowing orange.

Newt rolls along the floor—the Erumpent copies, moving nearer and nearer to the open case.

> NEWT
> Good girl—come on—into
> the case . . .

Jacob takes a sniff of the Erumpent musk. As he does so, a fish flies through the air and jolts him, spilling the musk.

The wind changes. Trees rustle. The Erumpent takes a deep breath in—she can smell the new, more powerful aroma coming from Jacob.

Jacob looks around. A seal sits behind him looking guilty, before cheekily running away.

When Jacob turns back, he sees the Erumpent is now on her feet, staring at him.

ANGLE ON NEWT AND JACOB, *realizing what is about to happen.*

BACK TO SCENE:

The Erumpent charges toward the source of the smell, bellowing madly. Jacob wails, running as fast as he can in the opposite direction. The Erumpent gives chase—they crash through rubble and ice ponds before charging across the snow-covered park.

Newt draws his wand—

> NEWT
>
> *Repar—*

Before he can finish, his wand is whipped out of his hand by a baboon, which runs off, clutching its prize.

> NEWT
> Merlin's beard!

ANGLE ON JACOB, tanking along, the Erumpent close behind him.

ANGLE ON NEWT, face-to-face with the curious baboon, which examines his wand.

Newt breaks a bit of twig off from a branch and holds it out, trying to persuade the baboon to trade with him.

> NEWT
> They're exactly the same . . .
> Same thing.

BACK TO JACOB: In trying to climb a tree, Jacob has ended up hanging precariously upside down from a branch.

> JACOB
> (bellowing, terrified)
> Newt!

We see the Erumpent below him. She lies on her back, wiggling her legs in the air invitingly.

ANGLE BACK ON NEWT: The baboon shakes Newt's wand.

NEWT
No, no, no, don't!

Newt looks worried—BANG—the wand "goes off," the spell knocking the baboon backward. The wand flies back to Newt.

NEWT
I'm so sorry—

ANGLE ON JACOB: The Erumpent is now on her feet. She charges toward the tree, digging her horn deep into the trunk. The tree bubbles with glowing liquid before exploding and crashing to the ground.

Jacob is thrown off, rolling down a steep, snowy hill, and onto the frozen lake below.

The Erumpent charges after him, hits the ice, and skids. Newt comes careering down the hill, also hitting the ice. He performs an athletic slide, his case open—the Erumpent is mere feet from Jacob when the case swallows her.

NEWT
Good show, Mr. Kowalski!

Jacob holds out his hand to shake.

JACOB
Call me Jacob.

They shake hands.

*THIRD-PERSON POV—Someone watches as Newt hauls
Jacob up and they slip and slide across the frozen lake as
fast as they can.*

NEWT
Well, two down—one to go.

*HOLD ON TINA as she hides on the bridge above them,
peeking down.*

NEWT (O.S.)
(to Jacob)
In you hop.

We see the case sitting alone below the bridge.

*Tina quickly appears around the corner and hurriedly
sits on the case. She closes the catches, looking shocked but
determined.*

ANNOUNCER (V.O.)
Ladies and gentlemen . . .

SCENE 55
INT. CITY HALL—NIGHT

A large ornately decorated hall, covered in patriotic emblems. Hundreds of glamorously dressed people sit at round tables, looking toward a stage at the far end. Over this stage hangs a large poster of Senator Shaw with a slogan reading AMERICA'S FUTURE.

An announcer stands behind the microphone.

ANNOUNCER
. . . now, tonight's key-note speaker needs no introduction from me. He's been mentioned as a future president—and if you don't believe me, just read his daddy's newspapers—

Indulgent laughter from the crowd. We see Shaw Sr. and Langdon seated at a table surrounded by the crème de la crème of New York society.

> ANNOUNCER
> —ladies and gentlemen, I
> give you the senator for New
> York, Henry Shaw!

Tumultuous applause. Senator Shaw bounds forward, acknowledging the cheers, pointing and winking at intimates in the crowd, and mounts the steps.

SCENE 56
EXT. DARK STREET—NIGHT

Something is streaking through the streets, too large and fast for a human. Strange, labored breathing and snarling—it is inhuman, beast-like.

SCENE 57
EXT. STREET NEAR CITY HALL—NIGHT

Tina is hurrying along, clutching the case. Streetlights start going out around her. She stops, feels something pass in the darkness—turns, staring, scared.

SCENE 58
INT. CITY HALL—NIGHT

> SENATOR SHAW
> . . . and it's true we have made
> some progress, but there is no
> reward for idleness. So just as
> the odious saloons have been
> banished . . .

A strange, haunting noise comes from the organ pipes at the back of the room. Everyone turns to look, the senator pauses.

> SENATOR SHAW
> . . . so now the pool halls, and
> these private parlors . . .

The strange noise gets louder.

Guests turn to look again. The senator seems anxious. People mutter.

Suddenly something explodes forth from underneath the organ. Something huge and bestial, although invisible, is soaring down the hall—tables fly, people are thrown, lights smash, and people scream as it carves a line toward the stage.

Senator Shaw is thrown backward against his own poster, raised up high, suspended for a moment in midair, before being brought down with a violent crash—dead.

The "beast" rips at his poster—a frenzied slashing with harsh, noisy breathing—before swarming back out from where it came.

Sounds of anguish and panic from the crowd as Shaw Sr. fights through the debris toward his son's torn and bleeding body.

ANGLE ON SENATOR SHAW'S BODY, his face brutally scarred. Shaw Sr. looks devastated as he crouches beside his son.

ANGLE ON LANGDON, now on his feet, slightly drunk. Determined, perhaps triumphant:

> LANGDON
> WITCHES!

SCENE 59
INT. MACUSA LOBBY—NIGHT

*Focus on the gigantic dial showing the Magical Exposure
Threat Level. The hand moves from* SEVERE *to* EMERGENCY.

*Tina, case in hand, runs up the lobby steps, past witches
and wizards huddled in groups, whispering nervously.*

> HEINRICH EBERSTADT (V.O.)
> Our American friends have
> permitted a breach of the
> Statute of Secrecy . . .

SCENE 60
INT. PENTAGRAM OFFICE—NIGHT

*An impressive hall arranged like an old parliament
debating chamber. Every seat is occupied by wizards from
all parts of the world. Madam Picquery is presiding, Graves
at her side.*

The Swiss delegate is speaking.

> HEINRICH EBERSTADT
> . . . that threatens to expose
> us all.

> MADAM PICQUERY
> I will not be lectured by
> the man who let Gellert
> Grindelwald slip through his
> fingers—

*A hologram image of Senator Shaw's dead and twisted body
floats high above the room, emitting a glowing light.*

All heads turn as Tina hurries into the chamber.

> TINA
> Madam President, I'm so
> sorry to interrupt, but this is
> critical—

*Echoing silence. Tina slides to a halt in the middle of the
marble floor before realizing exactly what she's walked
into. The delegates stare at her.*

> MADAM PICQUERY
> You'd better have an excellent
> excuse for this intrusion,
> Miss Goldstein.

> TINA
> Yes—I do.
>> *(stepping forward to
>> address her)*
> Ma'am. Yesterday a wizard
> entered New York with
> a case. This case full of
> magical creatures, and—
> unfortunately—some have
> escaped.

MADAM PICQUERY
He arrived yesterday? You
have known for twenty-four
hours that an unregistered
wizard set magical beasts
loose in New York and you
see fit to tell us only when a
man has been killed?

TINA
Who has been killed?

MADAM PICQUERY
Where is this man?

*Tina sets the case flat on the floor and thumps the lid. After
a second or two, it creaks open. First Newt, then Jacob
emerges, looking sheepish and nervous.*

BRITISH ENVOY
Scamander?

NEWT
(*closing the case*)
Oh—er—hello, Minister.

MOMOLU WOTORSON
Theseus Scamander? The war
hero?

BRITISH ENVOY
No, this is his little brother.
And what in the name of
Merlin are you doing in New
York?

NEWT
I came to buy an Appaloosa
Puffskein, sir.

BRITISH ENVOY
(*suspicious*)
Right. What are you really
doing here?

MADAM PICQUERY
(*to Tina, about Jacob*)
Goldstein—and who is this?

TINA
This is Jacob Kowalski,
Madam President, he's a No-
Maj who got bitten by one of
Mr. Scamander's creatures.

*Furious reaction from the MACUSA employees and
dignitaries all around.*

MINISTERS
(*whispers*)
No-Maj? Obliviated?

*Newt is absorbed in the image of Senator Shaw's body
floating around the room.*

> NEWT
> Merlin's beard.

> MADAM YA ZHOU
> You know which of your
> creatures was responsible,
> Mr. Scamander?

> NEWT
> No creature did this . . . Don't
> pretend! You must know what
> that was; look at the marks . . .

ANGLE ON SENATOR SHAW'S FACE.

ANGLE ON NEWT.

> NEWT
> That was an Obscurus.

Mass consternation, muttering, exclamations. Graves looks alert.

> MADAM PICQUERY
> You go too far, Mr. Scamander.
> There is no Obscurial in
> America. Impound that case,
> Graves!

*Graves summons the case; it lands next to him. Newt
draws his wand.*

> NEWT
> *(to Graves)*
> No ... Give that b—!

> MADAM PICQUERY
> Arrest them!

*A dazzling eruption of spells hits Newt, Tina, and Jacob, all
of whom are slammed to their knees. Newt's wand flies out
of his hands, caught by Graves.*

Graves stands and picks up the case.

> NEWT
> *(magically restrained)*
> No—no—don't hurt those
> creatures—please, you don't
> understand—nothing in there
> is dangerous, nothing!

> MADAM PICQUERY
> We'll be the judges of that!
> *(to the Aurors now
> standing behind them)*
> Take them to the cells!

ANGLE ON GRAVES watching Tina as she, Newt, and Jacob are dragged away—

> NEWT
> *(screaming, desperate)*
> Don't hurt those creatures—
> there is nothing in there that
> is dangerous. Please don't
> hurt my creatures—they are
> not dangerous . . . Please, they
> are not dangerous!

SCENE 61
INT. MACUSA CELL—DAY

Newt, Tina, and Jacob sitting, Newt with his head in his hands, still in utter despair about his creatures. Finally Tina, on the verge of tears, breaks the silence.

> TINA
> I am so sorry about your
> creatures, Mr. Scamander. I
> truly am.

Newt remains silent.

JACOB
(sotto voce, to Tina)
Can someone please tell
me what this Obscurial—
Obscurius thing is? Please?

TINA
(also sotto voce)
There hasn't been one for
centuries—

NEWT
I met one in Sudan three
months ago. There used to
be more of them but they
still exist. Before wizards
went underground, when
we were still being hunted
by Muggles, young wizards
and witches sometimes tried
to suppress their magic to
avoid persecution. Instead
of learning to harness or to
control their powers, they
developed what was called
an Obscurus.

TINA
(off Jacob's confusion)
It's an unstable, uncontrollable

Dark force that busts out
and—and attacks . . . and then
vanishes . . .

*As she talks, we see the penny dropping. An Obscurus fits
everything she knows about the perpetrator of the New
York attacks.*

> TINA
> *(to Newt)*
> Obscurials can't survive long,
> can they?

> NEWT
> There's no documented case
> of any Obscurial surviving
> past the age of ten. The one I
> met in Africa was eight when
> she—she was eight when she
> died.

> JACOB
> What are you telling me
> here—that Senator Shaw was
> killed by a—by a *kid*?

Newt's look says yes.

SCENE 62
INT. SECOND SALEM CHURCH, MAIN HALL—MONTAGE—DAY

Modesty approaches the long table at which many orphan children sit hungrily eating.

> MODESTY
> *(continuing her chant)*
> . . . My momma, your momma,
> flying on a switch,
> My momma, your momma,
> witches never cry,

> My momma, your momma,
> witches gonna die!

Modesty gathers several of the children's leaflets from the table.

                    MODESTY
           Witch number one, drown in
              a river!
           Witch number two, gotta
              noose to give her!
           Witch number three . . .

TIME CUT:

The children, having finished their meal, leave the table with their leaflets and head for the door.

                    CHASTITY
                (calling after them)
           Hand out your leaflets! I'll
           know if you dump 'em.
           Tell me if you see anything
           suspicious.

CLOSE ON CREDENCE—he's washing dishes, but watching the children intently.

Modesty follows the last of the children out of the church.

SCENE 63
EXT. STREET OUTSIDE SECOND SALEM
CHURCH—DAY

Modesty stands in the middle of the busy street. She throws her leaflets high into the air, watching with glee as they fall around her.

SCENE 64
INT. MACUSA CELL/CORRIDOR—DAY

Two executioners in white coats lead a shackled Newt and Tina down to a dark basement, away from the cell.

Newt turns to look back.

NEWT
(*over his shoulder*)
It was good to make your

acquaintance, Jacob, and I
hope you get your bakery.

*ANGLE ON JACOB, scared, left behind, clutching at the
bars of the cell. He waves forlornly after Newt.*

SCENE 65
INT. INTERROGATION ROOM—DAY

A small, bare room, black-walled and windowless.

*Graves sits opposite Newt at an interrogation desk, a file
open in front of him. Newt squints forward, a bright light
shining into his eyes.*

Tina stands behind, flanked by the two executioners.

> GRAVES
> You're an interesting man,
> Mr. Scamander.

> TINA
> *(stepping forward)*
> Mr. Graves—

Graves holds a finger to his lips, signaling for Tina to be silent. The gesture is patronizing, but authoritative. Tina looks kowtowed—she obeys, stepping back into the shadows.

Graves examines the file on his desk.

> GRAVES
> You were thrown out of
> Hogwarts for endangering
> human life—

> NEWT
> That was an accident!

> GRAVES
> —with a beast. Yet one of
> your teachers argued strongly
> against your expulsion.
> Now, what makes Albus
> Dumbledore so fond of you?

> NEWT
> I really couldn't say.

> GRAVES
> So setting a pack of
> dangerous creatures loose
> here was just another
> accident, is that right?

NEWT
Why would I do it
deliberately?

GRAVES
To expose wizardkind. To
provoke war between the
magical and non-magical
worlds.

NEWT
Mass slaughter for the greater
good, you mean?

GRAVES
Yes. Quite.

NEWT
I'm not one of Grindelwald's
fanatics, Mr. Graves.

A tiny change of expression tells us that Newt has scored a hit. Graves is looking more menacing.

GRAVES
I wonder what you can
tell me about this, Mr.
Scamander?

With a slow move of his hand, Graves raises up the

*Obscurus from Newt's case. He brings it onto the desk—it
is pulsing, swirling, and hissing.*

CLOSE ON TINA as she stares, disbelieving.

*Graves reaches a hand toward the Obscurus—he's utterly
fascinated. At his sudden close proximity, the Obscurus
swirls faster, bubbling and shrinking backward.*

*Newt turns instinctively to Tina. Without fully realizing
why, it is she whom he wants to convince.*

> NEWT
> It's an Obscurus—
> *(off her look)*
> But it's not what you think. I
> managed to separate it from
> the Sudanese girl as I tried to
> save her—I wanted to take it
> home, to study it—
> *(off Tina's shock)*
> But it cannot survive outside
> that box, it could not hurt
> anyone, Tina!

> GRAVES
> So it's useless without the
> host?

NEWT
"Useless?" "Useless?" That is a
parasitical magical force that
killed a child. What on earth
would you use it for?

Newt, anger finally boiling within him, stares at Graves.
Tina, reacting to the atmosphere, also looks to Graves—
concern and trepidation written across her face.

Graves realizes his mistake. He stands, brushing off the
questions, turning the blame back onto Newt.

GRAVES
You fool nobody, Mr.
Scamander. You brought
this Obscurus into the city
of New York in the hope of
causing mass disruption—
breaking the Statute of
Secrecy and revealing the
magical world—

NEWT
You know that can't hurt
anyone, you know that!

GRAVES
—you are therefore guilty
of a treasonous betrayal of

your fellow wizards and are
sentenced to death. Miss
Goldstein, who has aided and
abetted you—

NEWT
No, she's done nothing of the
kind—

GRAVES
—she receives the same
sentence.

*The two executioners step forward. They calmly,
intrusively, press the tips of their wands into Newt's and
Tina's necks.*

*Tina is so overcome with shock and fear that she can barely
speak.*

GRAVES
(to the executioners)
Just do it immediately. I will
inform President Picquery
myself.

NEWT
Tina.

Graves again places a finger to his lips.

GRAVES
      Shh.
                (*waving to the
                  executioners*)
      Please.

SCENE 66
INT. SHABBY BASEMENT MEETING ROOM—DAY

Queenie is carrying a tray of coffee and mugs toward a meeting room.

Suddenly she freezes, her eyes widen, a look of terror across her face. She drops the tray—cups smashing on the floor.

An assortment of low-level MACUSA functionaries turn to stare at her. Queenie stares back, stunned, before running away down the corridor.

SCENE 67
INT. CORRIDOR LEADING TO DEATH CELL—
DAY

A long, black, metallic corridor leads into a pure white cell,
which consists of a chair suspended magically over a square
pool of rippling potion.

Newt and Tina are forced into this room by the
executioners. A guard stands at the door.

> TINA
> *(to the executioner)*
> Don't do this—Bernadette—
> please—

> EXECUTIONER 1
> It don't hurt.

Tina is led to the edge of the pool. She begins panicking, her
breathing heavy and erratic.

The smiling executioner raises a wand and carefully
extracts Tina's happy memories from her head. Tina
instantly calms—her expression now vacant, otherworldly.

*The executioner casts the memories into the potion, which
ripples, coming alive with scenes from Tina's life:*

A young Tina smiles up as her mother calls:

> TINA'S MOTHER (V.O.)
> Tina . . . Tina . . . Come on,
> pumpkin—time for bed. Are
> you ready?

> TINA
> Momma . . .

*Tina's mother appears in the pool, her expression loving
and warm. The real Tina watches, smiling down.*

> EXECUTIONER 1
> Don't that look good. You
> wanna get in? Huh?

Tina nods vacantly.

SCENE 68
INT. MACUSA LOBBY—DAY

Queenie stands in the crowded lobby.

The elevator doors sound.

ANGLE ON THE ELEVATOR DOORS, which open, revealing Jacob, escorted by Sam, the Obliviator.

Queenie hurries toward them, determined.

> QUEENIE
> Hey, Sam!

> SAM
> Hey, Queenie.

> QUEENIE
> They need you downstairs.
> I'll Obliviate this guy.

> SAM
> You ain't qualified.

Grim-faced, Queenie reads his mind.

> QUEENIE
> Hey, Sam—does Cecily know
> you been seeing Ruby?

ANGLE ON RUBY, a MACUSA witch, standing ahead of them. She smiles at Sam.

ANGLE ON QUEENIE AND SAM—Sam looks nervous.

> SAM
> *(appalled)*
> How'd you—?

> QUEENIE
> Let me Obliviate this guy
> and she'll never hear about it
> from me.

Stunned, Sam backs away. Queenie seizes Jacob's arm and marches him off across the cavernous lobby.

> JACOB
> What are you doin'?

> QUEENIE
> Shh! Teen's in trouble, I'm
> trying to listen—
> *(she reads Tina's mind)*
> Jacob, where's Newt's case?

> JACOB
> I think that guy Graves took
> it—

> QUEENIE
> Okay, come on—

> JACOB
> What? You're not gonna
> Obliviate me?

> QUEENIE
> Of course not—you're one of
> us now!

Queenie hurries him toward the main staircase.

SCENE 69
INT. DEATH CELL—DAY

Tina sits in the execution chair. She gazes down: Beneath her swirl happy images of her family, her parents, a young Queenie.

MEMORY:

We move into the pool and follow one of Tina's memories: Tina walks inside the Second Salem church and up the stairs. She finds Mary Lou, standing over Credence, belt

in hand—Credence looks terrified. In anger, Tina casts a spell, striking Mary Lou. Tina moves forward to comfort Credence:

> TINA
> It's okay.

ANGLE BACK ON REAL TINA, still gazing into the pool, smiling wistfully.

ANGLE ON NEWT, who glances quickly down his own arm—Pickett is clambering, quiet and agile, toward the shackles holding Newt's hands.

SCENE 70
INT. CORRIDOR LEADING TO GRAVES'S OFFICE—DAY

ANGLE ON THE DOOR TO GRAVES'S OFFICE.

> QUEENIE (O.S.)
> Alohomora.

We see Queenie and Jacob standing awkwardly outside Graves's office, Queenie trying desperately to open the door.

QUEENIE

Aberto . . .

The door remains locked.

QUEENIE
(frustrated)
Ugh. He would know a fancy
spell to lock his office.

SCENE 71
INT. DEATH CELL—DAY

*Back to Pickett as he finishes unlocking the shackles holding
Newt's wrists, and quickly climbs onto Executioner 2's coat.*

EXECUTIONER 2
(to Newt)
Okay, let's get the good stuff
out of you—

*Executioner 2 raises her wand to Newt's forehead. Newt
seizes his opportunity—he jumps backward out of the
way before revealing the Swooping Evil, which he throws
forward toward the pool. He then swiftly turns and punches
the guard, knocking him out cold.*

The Swooping Evil has now expanded into a gigantic, spooky, but weirdly beautiful butterfly-esque reptile with skeletal wings. It continues to circle round and round the pool.

Pickett clambers onto Executioner 2's arm and bites, startling and distracting her, giving Newt time to grab her arms and take aim with her wand. A spell fires, hitting Executioner 1, who drops to the floor, her wand falling into the pool. As it falls, the liquid rises up in viscous black bubbles, instantly engulfing the wand.

In reaction, Tina's memories turn from good to bad: We see Mary Lou, pointing aggressively at Tina:

MARY LOU

Witch!

Tina, still enraptured by the pool, looks increasingly terrified. Her stool is lowering closer and closer to the liquid.

The Swooping Evil glides across the room, knocking Executioner 2 to the ground.

SCENE 72
INT. CORRIDOR LEADING TO GRAVES'S
OFFICE—DAY

After a quick glance around, Jacob gives the door a hefty kick. It breaks open.

Jacob stands guard as Queenie runs in and grabs Newt's case and Tina's wand.

SCENE 73
INT. DEATH CELL—DAY

Tina snaps out of her reverie and screams:

TINA

MR. SCAMANDER!

The liquid has now turned to a black bubbling death potion. It rises up, surrounding Tina on her chair, almost engulfing her. Tina stands up to get away, almost falling off in her haste. She tries desperately to regain her balance.

NEWT

DON'T PANIC!

TINA
WHAT DO YOU SUGGEST
I DO INSTEAD?

*Newt makes a strange tutting sound, commanding the
Swooping Evil to circle the pool once more.*

NEWT
Jump . . .

Tina looks at the Swooping Evil—fearful, disbelieving.

TINA
ARE YOU CRAZY?

NEWT
Jump on him.

*Newt stands on the edge of the pool, watching the Swooping
Evil as it circles round and round Tina.*

NEWT
Tina, listen to me. I'll catch
you. Tina!

*The two make intense eye contact, Newt trying to
reassure . . .*

*The liquid has now risen up in waves to Tina's full height—
she's losing sight of Newt.*

NEWT
(insistent, very calm)
I'll catch you. I've got you,
Tina . . .

Suddenly Newt cries out:

NEWT
Go!

Tina jumps in between two of the waves, just as the Swooping Evil passes. She lands on its back, only inches away from the swirling liquid, then hops quickly forward, straight into Newt's open arms.

For a split second, Newt and Tina gaze at each other, before Newt raises his hand, recalling the Swooping Evil, which folds into a cocoon once more.

Newt grabs Tina's hand and heads for the exit.

NEWT
Come on!

SCENE 74
INT. DEATH CELL CORRIDOR—DAY

Queenie and Jacob march along the corridor with purpose.

An alarm goes off in the distance—other wizards hurry past them in the opposite direction.

SCENE 75
INT. MACUSA LOBBY—MINUTES LATER—DAY

The alarm blares out across the lobby.

Confusion reigns among the crowd—people gather in groups, nervously chattering, others scurry about, urgent, anxious.

A team of Aurors hurtles across the lobby, headed directly for the stairs leading down to the basement.

SCENE 76
INT. DEATH CELL CORRIDOR/BASEMENT
CORRIDOR—DAY

Newt and Tina, hand in hand, charge through the basement corridors.

Suddenly accosted by the group of Aurors, they turn, darting behind pillars, just missing the fired curses and spells.

Newt again sends out the Swooping Evil, which swirls overhead, flying in and out of pillars, blocking curses and knocking Aurors to the ground.

ANGLE ON THE SWOOPING EVIL using its proboscis to probe in one of the Aurors' ears.

> NEWT
> *(making a clicking sound)*
> LEAVE HIS BRAINS, come
> on! Come on!

Tina and Newt run onward, the Swooping Evil flying after, blocking curses as it goes.

> TINA
> What *is* that thing?

> NEWT
> Swooping Evil.

TINA

Well, I love it!

ANGLE ON QUEENIE AND JACOB, walking briskly through the basement. Newt and Tina sprint around the corner and almost collide with them. The four stare at one another, panic on all their faces.

Finally, Queenie gestures to the case:

QUEENIE

Get in!

SCENE 77
INT. STAIRS LEADING TO CELLS—MOMENTS LATER—DAY

Graves moves down the stairs with urgency. For the first time, a look of panic on his face.

SCENE 78
INT. MACUSA LOBBY—MINUTES LATER—DAY

Queenie moves quickly across the lobby floor, trying desperately not to be conspicuous in her haste, but acutely aware of the need to leave.

A flustered Abernathy emerges from a crowd of wizards.

> ABERNATHY
> Queenie!

Queenie, poised at the top of the stairs, turns and composes herself.

Abernathy moves toward her, straightening his tie, trying to appear calm and authoritative—Queenie obviously makes him nervous.

> ABERNATHY
> *(a large smile)*
> Where you going?

Queenie puts on an alluringly innocent expression and holds the case behind her back.

> QUEENIE
> I'm . . . I'm sick, Mr.
> Abernathy.

She coughs a little, widening her eyes.

> ABERNATHY
> Again? Well—what've you got
> there?

A beat.

*Queenie thinks fast, her face quickly breaking into a
breathtaking smile.*

> QUEENIE
> Ladies' things.

*Queenie produces the case and innocently trots up the steps
toward Abernathy.*

> QUEENIE
> You wanna take a look? I
> don't mind.

Abernathy is overcome with embarrassment.

> ABERNATHY
> (swallowing hard)
> Oh! Good gravy, no! I—you
> get well now!

QUEENIE
(*smiling sweetly and
arranging his tie*)
Thanks!

*Queenie immediately turns and hurries down the stairs,
leaving Abernathy—heart racing—staring after her.*

SCENE 79
EXT. STREETS OF NEW YORK—LATE AFTERNOON

HIGH WIDE ABOVE NEW YORK. We zoom over rooftops before diving down through streets and alleyways, past speeding cars and cackling children.

We come to rest in an alleyway at the Second Salem Church, where Credence is pasting up posters advertising Mary Lou's next meeting.

Graves Apparates into the alleyway. Credence, startled, backs away, but Graves makes straight for him, his tone and manner urgent, forceful.

GRAVES

Credence. Have you found
the child?

CREDENCE

I can't.

*Graves, impatient but feigning calm, holds out his hand—
suddenly seeming caring, affectionate:*

GRAVES

Show me.

*Credence whimpers and cowers, almost backing farther
away. Graves gently takes Credence's hand in his own and
examines it—the hand is covered in deep red cuts, sore and
bleeding.*

GRAVES

Shhhh. My boy, the sooner
we find this child, the sooner
you can put that pain in the
past where it belongs.

*Graves gently, almost seductively, moves his thumb across
the cuts, healing them instantly. Credence stares.*

*Graves seems to make a decision. He puts on an earnest,
trustworthy expression as, from his pocket, he produces a
chain bearing the symbol of the Deathly Hallows.*

GRAVES
I want you to have this,
Credence. I would trust very
few with it—

Graves moves close, placing the chain around Credence's neck as he whispers:

GRAVES
Very few.

Graves places his hands on either side of Credence's neck, drawing him in, his speech quiet, intimate:

GRAVES
. . . But you—you're different.

Credence is unsure, both nervous of and attracted by Graves's behavior.

Graves rests his hand on Credence's heart, covering the pendant.

GRAVES
Now, when you find the
child, touch this symbol and
I will know, and I will come
to you.

Graves moves even closer to Credence, his face inches from

the boy's neck—the effect is both alluring and threatening—
as he whispers:

> GRAVES
> Do this and you will be
> honored among wizards.
> Forever.

Graves pulls Credence into a hug, which, with his hand on
Credence's neck, seems more controlling than affectionate.
Credence, overwhelmed by the seeming affection, closes his
eyes and relaxes slightly.

Graves slowly backs away, stroking Credence's neck.
Credence keeps his eyes closed, longing for the human
contact to continue.

> GRAVES
> *(whispers)*
> The child is dying, Credence.
> Time is running out.

Abruptly, Graves strides back down the alleyway and
Disapparates.

SCENE 80
EXT. ROOFTOP WITH PIGEON COOP—DUSK

A rooftop overlooking the whole city. In the middle sits a small wooden shed, which houses a pigeon coop.

Newt steps up onto a ledge and stands looking over the immense city. Pickett sits on his shoulder, clicking.

Jacob is inside the shed looking at the pigeon coop as Queenie enters.

> QUEENIE
> Your grandfather kept
> pigeons? Mine bred owls. I
> used to love feeding 'em.

ANGLE ON NEWT AND TINA—Tina has joined Newt in standing on the ledge.

> TINA
> Graves always insisted the
> disturbances were caused
> by a beast. We need to catch
> all your creatures so he
> can't keep using them as a
> scapegoat.

> NEWT
> There's only one still missing.

Dougal, my Demiguise.

                    TINA
Dougal?

                    NEWT
Slight problem is that . . . um,
he's invisible.

                    TINA
          (this is so ridiculous that
          she can't help but smile)
Invisible?

                    NEWT
Yes—most of the time . . . he
does . . . um . . .

                    TINA
How do you catch something
that—?

                    NEWT
          (beginning to smile)
With immense difficulty.

                    TINA
Oh . . .

They smile at each other—there's a new warmth between

them, Newt still awkward but somehow unable to stop staring at Tina as she smiles.

Tina moves slowly toward Newt.

A beat.

                    TINA
          Gnarlak!

                    NEWT
               (taken aback)
          Excuse me?

                    TINA
          (conspiratorial, excited)
          Gnarlak—he was an
          informant of mine when I
          was an Auror! He used to
          trade in magical creatures on
          the side—

                    NEWT
          He wouldn't happen to have
          an interest in paw prints,
          would he?

                    TINA
          He's interested in anything he
          can sell.

SCENE 81
EXT. THE BLIND PIG—NIGHT

Tina leads the group down an insalubrious back alley covered in bins, crates, and discarded objects. She locates a set of steps leading to a basement apartment and motions them down.

The steps appear to lead to a dead end: The doorway has been bricked up. Instead, a poster of a simpering debutante in evening dress, gazing at herself in a mirror, covers the end of the walkway.

Tina and Queenie stand in front of this poster. They turn to each other and, in unison, raise their wands. As they do so, their work clothes transform into stunning flapper party dresses. Tina looks up at Newt, somewhat embarrassed by her new attire. Queenie gazes at Jacob, a cheeky smile on her face.

Tina steps toward the poster and slowly raises her hand. As she does so, the eyes of the debutante move upward, following her every move. Tina knocks slowly on the door four times.

Newt, sensing the need for a change, hastily magics himself a small bow tie. Jacob looks on, jealously.

A hatch opens: The painted eyes of the debutante whip back to reveal the gaze of a suspicious guard.

SCENE 82
INT. THE BLIND PIG—NIGHT

A seedy, low-ceilinged speakeasy for the down-and-out of New York's magical community. Every witch and wizard criminal in New York is here, their wanted posters hanging proudly on the walls. A glimpse of GELLERT GRINDELWALD: WANTED FOR NO-MAJ SLAYINGS IN EUROPE.

A glamorous goblin jazz singer croons on a stage full of goblin musicians, smoky images wafting from her wand to illustrate her lyrics. All is dingy and shabby, an atmosphere of menacing fun.

> JAZZ SINGER
> The phoenix cried fat tears of
>   pearl
> When the dragon snapped up
>   his best girl,
> And the Billywig forgot to
>   twirl
> When his sweetheart left him
>   cold,
> And the unicorn done lost his
>   horn,
> And the Hippogriff feels all
>   forlorn,
> 'Cause their lady loves have
>   upped and gawn,
> Or that's what I've been
>   told—

Jacob stands at the seemingly unmanned bar, waiting to be served.

> JACOB
> How do I get a drink in this
> joint?

Out of nowhere, a thin bottle of brown liquid zooms toward him. He catches it, stunned.

The head of a house-elf peers up at him from behind the bar.

> HOUSE-ELF
> What? Ain't you ever seen a
> house-elf before?

> JACOB
> Oh, no, yeah, no, yeah, of
> course I have . . . I love house-
> elves.

Jacob tries to act nonchalant—he removes the cork from the bottle.

> JACOB
> My uncle's a house-elf.

The house-elf—not fooled—raises himself up, leaning on the bar to stare at Jacob.

Queenie approaches. She looks downcast as she orders:

> QUEENIE
> Six shots of gigglewater and a
> lobe blaster, please.

The house-elf reluctantly shuffles off to fulfill her request.

Jacob and Queenie look at each other. Jacob reaches out and takes one of the gigglewater shots.

QUEENIE
Are all No-Majs like you?

JACOB
*(trying to be serious,
almost seductive)*
No, I'm the only one like me.

Maintaining strong eye contact with Queenie, Jacob knocks back the shot. Suddenly he emits a raucous, high-pitched giggle. Queenie laughs sweetly at his look of surprise.

ANGLE ON A HOUSE-ELF serving a drink to a giant, whose hand dwarfs the mug he is handed.

ANGLE ON NEWT AND TINA sitting at a table alone. There's an awkward silence. Newt studies the characters in the room: Hooded and heavily scarred witches and wizards gamble magical artifacts in a game with runic dice.

TINA
(looking around)
I've arrested half of the
people in here.

NEWT
You can tell me to mind my

own business . . . but I saw
something in that death
potion back there. I saw
you—hugging—that Second
Salem boy.

                    TINA
His name's Credence. His
mother beats him. She beats all
those kids she adopted, but she
seems to hate him the most.

                    NEWT
                (realizing)
And she was the No-Maj you
attacked?

                    TINA
That's how I lost my job.
I went for her in front of
a meeting of her crazy
followers—they all had to
be Obliviated. It was a big
scandal.

Queenie signals from across the room:

                    QUEENIE
                (whispers)
It's him.

*Gnarlak has emerged from the depths of the speakeasy.
Smoking a cigar and smartly dressed for a goblin, he has
a sly, smooth demeanor like a Mafia boss. He eyes the
newcomers as he walks.*

> JAZZ SINGER (O.S.)
> Yes, love has set the beasts
>   astir,
> The dang'rous and the meek
>   concur,
> It's ruffled feathers, fleece,
>   and fur,
> 'Cause love drives all of us
>   wild.

*Gnarlak sits himself at the end of their table, an air of
confidence and dangerous control. A house-elf hastily
brings him a drink.*

> GNARLAK
> So—you're the guy with the
> case full of monsters, huh?

> NEWT
> News travels fast. I was
> hoping you'd be able to tell
> me if there have been any
> sightings. Tracks. That sort of
> thing.

Gnarlak downs his drink. Another house-elf brings him a document to sign.

> GNARLAK
> You've got a big price on your
> head, Mr. Scamander. Why
> should I help you instead of
> turnin' you in?

> NEWT
> I take it I'll have to make it
> worth your while?

The house-elf scurries off holding the signed document.

> GNARLAK
> Hmm—let's consider it a
> cover charge.

Newt pulls out a couple of Galleons and slides them across the table toward Gnarlak, who barely looks up.

> GNARLAK
> (not impressed)
> Huh—MACUSA's offerin'
> more'n that.

A beat.

Newt pulls out a beautiful metal instrument and places it on the table.

GNARLAK
Lunascope? I got five.

Newt rummages in his coat pocket and pulls out a glowing, frozen ruby egg instead.

NEWT
Frozen Ashwinder egg!

GNARLAK
(finally interested)
You see—now we're—

Gnarlak suddenly spots Pickett, who is peeking out of Newt's pocket.

GNARLAK
—wait a minute—that's a
Bowtruckle, right?

Pickett quickly retreats and Newt puts a hand protectively over his pocket.

NEWT
No.

GNARLAK
Ah, come on, that's a
Bowtruckle—they pick
locks—am I right?

NEWT
You're not having him.

GNARLAK
Well, good luck gettin' back
alive, Mr. Scamander, what
with the whole of MACUSA
on your back.

Gnarlak gets up and walks away.

NEWT
(in agony)
All right.

Gnarlak, turned away from Newt, smiles viciously.

*Newt extracts Pickett from his pocket. Pickett clings to
Newt's hands, madly clicking and whining.*

NEWT
Pickett . . .

*Newt slowly hands Pickett over to Gnarlak. Pickett reaches
his little arms forward, imploring Newt to take him back.
Newt cannot look at him.*

GNARLAK
(regarding Pickett)
Ah yeah . . .

(to Newt)
Somethin' invisible's been
wreakin' havoc around Fifth
Avenue. You may wanna
check out Macy's department
store. Might help with what
you're looking for.

NEWT
(sotto voce)
Dougal . . .
(to Gnarlak)
Right, one last thing. There's
a Mr. Graves who works at
MACUSA—I was wondering
what you knew of his
background.

Gnarlak stares. A sense that there is much that he could
say—and that he'd rather die than say it.

GNARLAK
You ask too many questions,
Mr. Scamander. That can get
you killed.

ANGLE ON A HOUSE-ELF carrying a crate of bottles.

HOUSE-ELF
MACUSA ARE COMING!

The house-elf Disapparates. Other customers throughout the bar hurriedly do the same.

TINA
(getting to her feet)
You tipped them off!

Gnarlak stares at them, chuckling menacingly.

Behind Queenie, the wanted posters on the wall update to show Newt's and Tina's faces.

Aurors begin Apparating into the speakeasy.

Jacob, seemingly innocent, saunters up to Gnarlak.

JACOB
Sorry, Mr. Gnarlak—

Jacob punches Gnarlak straight in the face, knocking him backward. Queenie looks delighted.

JACOB
—reminds me of my foreman!

Throughout the bar, various customers are being apprehended by the Aurors.

Newt scrambles about on the floor looking for Pickett. Around him, people are running, diving away from Aurors,

*trying to escape the bar. Newt finally finds Pickett on a
table leg, grabs him, and runs toward his group.*

*Jacob grabs another shot of gigglewater and knocks it back.
He giggles uproariously as Newt grabs his elbow and the
group Disapparates.*

SCENE 83
INT. SECOND SALEM CHURCH—NIGHT

*The long room is dimly lit by one set of lights. There's
barely any noise.*

*Chastity sits primly at the long table in the middle of the
church. She formulaically arranges leaflets and places them
in little bags.*

*Modesty sits opposite in a nightdress, reading a book. In the
deep background, Mary Lou busies herself in her bedroom.*

*Modesty is the only one to register a small clunk from
upstairs.*

SCENE 84
INT. MODESTY'S BEDROOM—NIGHT

A bleak room. A single bed, an oil lamp, a sampler on the wall: AN ALPHABET OF SIN. Modesty's dolls lined up on a shelf. One with a little noose around its neck, another tied to a stake.

Credence scrabbles to get underneath Modesty's bed. He looks among the boxes and objects hidden there, then suddenly stops, staring . . .

SCENE 85
INT. SECOND SALEM CHURCH—NIGHT

Modesty stands at the bottom of the stairs, looking up. She slowly ascends.

SCENE 86
INT. MODESTY'S BEDROOM—NIGHT

ANGLE ON CREDENCE'S FACE UNDER THE BED—
Credence has found a toy wand. He stares, unable to draw
his eyes from it.

Behind him, Modesty enters.

> MODESTY
> Whatchoo doin', Credence?

Credence bangs his head on the bed in his haste to get out. He
emerges, dusty and scared. He is relieved to see that it is only
Modesty, but she, on seeing the wand, is terrified.

> CREDENCE
> Where'd you get this?

> MODESTY
> *(frightened whisper)*
> Give it back, Credence. It's
> just a toy!

The door bangs open. Mary Lou enters. Her gaze travels
from Modesty to Credence and the toy wand—she is
angrier than we have ever seen her.

> MARY LOU
> *(to Credence)*
> What is this?

SCENE 87
INT. SECOND SALEM CHURCH—NIGHT

HOLD ON CHASTITY, still filling bags with leaflets.

> MARY LOU (O.S.)
> Take it off!

Chastity glances up toward the landing.

SCENE 88
INT. SECOND SALEM CHURCH, UPSTAIRS
LANDING—NIGHT

Mary Lou stands on the landing overlooking the main church below. Seen from below, her figure is powerful, almost deified.

Mary Lou turns back toward Credence and slowly, her face full of loathing, snaps the wand in two.

As Modesty cowers, Credence begins to remove his belt.
Mary Lou holds out her hand and takes it.

> CREDENCE
> *(pleading)*
> Ma . . .

> MARY LOU
> I am not your ma! Your
> mother was a wicked,
> unnatural woman!

Modesty forces her way between them.

> MODESTY
> It was mine.

> MARY LOU
> Modesty—

Suddenly—the belt is whipped out of Mary Lou's hands
by supernatural means and falls like a dead snake in a far
corner. Mary Lou looks at her hand—it is cut and bleeding
from the force of the movement.

Mary Lou is stunned—she glances between Modesty and
Credence.

MARY LOU
(*frightened but covering it*)
What is this?

Modesty stares defiantly directly back at her. In the background we see Credence crouched down, hugging his knees and shaking.

Trying to remain composed, Mary Lou moves slowly to retrieve the belt. Before she can touch it, the belt slithers away across the floor.

Mary Lou backs away, tears of fear welling in her eyes. She turns slowly back toward the children.

As she moves, an almighty force explodes into her: a bestial, screeching, dark mass that consumes her. Her scream is bloodcurdling as the force throws her backward, striking a wooden beam, flinging her over the balcony.

Mary Lou smashes down onto the floor of the main church, her body lifeless, her face bearing the same scars seen on the face of Senator Shaw.

The Dark force flies through the church, upending the table and destroying everything in sight.

SCENE 89
EXT. DEPARTMENT STORE—NIGHT

WIDE SHOT OF A DEPARTMENT STORE, its windows full of glamorously dressed mannequins.

Jacob approaches the shop windows, staring at a handbag which, seemingly of its own accord, is sliding down the arm of a mannequin. Newt, Tina, and Queenie hurry up behind him and watch as the bag hovers in midair and floats off into the store.

SCENE 90
INT. DEPARTMENT STORE—NIGHT

A well-presented department store decorated for Christmas, with aisles full of expensive jewelry, shoes, hats, and perfume. The place is shut down for the night, all the lights are off, no noises can be heard.

We see the handbag float down the central aisle, accompanied by small grunting noises.

Newt and the group quickly tiptoe through the store, coming to hide behind a large plastic Christmas display. They eye-up the floating handbag.

> NEWT
> *(whispers)*
> So Demiguises are
> fundamentally peaceful,
> but they can give a nasty
> nip if provoked.

The Demiguise itself appears—a silvery-haired orangutan-like creature, with a curious, wizened face—clambering over a display to reach a box of sweets.

NEWT
(to Jacob and Queenie)
You two . . . head that way.

They start moving.

NEWT
And try very hard not to be
predictable.

Jacob and Queenie exchange perplexed glances before heading off.

A small roar can be heard in the distance.

ANGLE ON THE DEMIGUISE, which, on hearing the sound, looks up toward the ceiling, before continuing to gather sweets, now shoveling them into its handbag.

TINA (O.S.)
(regarding the roar)
Was that the Demiguise?

NEWT
No, I think it might be the
reason that the Demiguise is
here.

ANGLE ON NEWT AND TINA, moving swiftly down an aisle toward the Demiguise, which is now moving away through the store.

Realizing it's been spotted, the Demiguise turns and looks at Newt quizzically before moving up a set of side stairs. Newt smiles and moves to follow.

SCENE 91
INT. DEPARTMENT STORE, ATTIC
STOREROOM—NIGHT

A huge, dark attic space, full floor to ceiling with shelves packed with boxes of china: dinner services, teacups, and general kitchenware.

The Demiguise walks along the attic in a patch of moonlight. It glances around before stopping and emptying its handbag full of confectionery.

> NEWT (O.S.)
> Its sight operates on
> probability, so it can foresee
> the most likely immediate
> future.

Newt comes into view, creeping up behind the Demiguise.

TINA (O.S.)
So what's it doing now?

NEWT
It's babysitting.

*The Demiguise holds up one of the sweets, seeming to offer
it up to someone or something.*

TINA
What did you just say—?

NEWT
(*calm and whispered*)
This is my fault. I thought I
had them all—but I must have
miscounted.

*Jacob and Queenie enter quietly. Newt moves calmly
forward and kneels beside the Demiguise, which makes
space for him in front of the sweets. Newt carefully places
his case down.*

*ANGLE ON TINA—a shift of light reveals the scales of a
large creature, hiding in the rafters of the attic. Tina looks
up in horror.*

TINA
It was babysitting that?

ANGLE ON THE CEILING as the face of an Occamy comes into view—just like the small, blue, snake-like birds seen in the case, but this Occamy is huge, coiled round and round itself to fill the entire attic roof space.

The Occamy moves slowly down toward Newt and the Demiguise, which again offers up a sweet. Newt remains very still.

> NEWT
> Occamies are choranaptyxic.
> So they—grow—to fill—
> available—space.

The Occamy spots Newt, and cranes its head toward him. Newt holds up a hand, gently:

> NEWT
> Mummy's here.

ANGLE ON THE DEMIGUISE, whose eyes flash a brilliant blue—a sign that it's having a premonition.

FLASH CUTS:

A Christmas bauble rolls across the floor; the Occamy is panicking, Newt clasping its back, being flung about the room; the Demiguise is suddenly on Jacob's back.

BACK TO THE DEMIGUISE as its eyes turn back to brown.

Queenie moves slowly forward, staring at the Occamy. As she does so, she accidentally kicks a tiny glass bauble on the floor, which jingles as it rolls. At the sound, the Occamy rears up, screeching. Newt tries to calm the large creature:

NEWT
Whoa! Whoa!

Jacob and Queenie stagger backward to find cover. The Demiguise runs away and jumps into Jacob's arms.

The Occamy swoops, scooping Newt up onto its back as it violently thrashes about the attic, sending shelves flying. Newt shouts out:

NEWT
Right, we need an insect, any
kind of insect—and a teapot!
Find a teapot!

Tina army-crawls through the chaos, dodging falling items, trying to find what Newt has asked for.

The wings of the Occamy crash down to the floor, narrowly missing Jacob as he stumbles around, encumbered by the Demiguise now clinging to his back.

Newt finds it harder and harder to hold on as the Occamy becomes more and more distressed, its wings now thrashing upward, destroying the roof of the building.

Jacob turns, he and the Demiguise spotting a stray cockroach on a crate. Jacob reaches his hand up to grab it, when part of the Occamy crashes down, destroying the crate and his chance.

ANGLE ON TINA, crawling across the floor with great determination, in hot pursuit of a cockroach.

ANGLE ON QUEENIE, who screams as she's knocked to the floor by the force of the Occamy. Jacob runs up behind her and dives forward, flat onto the floor, finally laying claim to a cockroach.

Tina stands clutching a teapot and screaming:

TINA

Teapot!

At this noise, the Occamy rears its head once more, causing its tail to writhe, squashing and pinning Jacob—with the Demiguise—against one of the rafters.

Jacob and Tina are now at opposite ends of the room, neither daring to move, swaths of Occamy scales between them.

ANGLE ON JACOB AND THE DEMIGUISE—the Demiguise looks shiftily up to the side and promptly vanishes. Jacob slowly turns to follow the Demiguise's gaze—the Occamy's face is inches away from his own, staring with full intensity at the cockroach in his hand. Jacob barely dares to breathe.

Newt peers around from behind the Occamy's head and whispers:

NEWT
Roach in teapot . . .

Jacob gulps, trying not to make eye contact with the huge creature next to him.

JACOB
*(trying to soothe the
Occamy)*
Shhhhh!

Jacob widens his eyes at Tina, warning her of his intent.

IN SLOW MOTION:

Jacob throws the roach. We watch it soar through the air as the Occamy's body begins to move once more, uncurling and swirling around the room.

Newt jumps from the Occamy's back, landing safely on the floor, while Queenie takes cover, placing a colander over her head.

Tina runs, teapot outstretched, hurdling the Occamy coils as she goes—an heroic sight. She lands on her knees in the center of the room, the cockroach falling perfectly into the teapot.

The Occamy rears up, shrinking rapidly as it rises, before diving down headfirst. Tina lowers her head, bracing herself for a hit. The Occamy races down toward the teapot and glides seamlessly inside.

Newt leaps forward and jams a lid on top of the teapot. He and Tina breathe heavily: relief.

> NEWT
>
> Choranaptyxic. They also
> *shrink* to fit the available
> space.

ANGLE INSIDE THE TEAPOT, the now tiny Occamy gobbling down its cockroach.

> TINA
>
> Tell me the truth—was that
> everything that came out of
> the case?

> NEWT
>
> That's everything—and that's
> the truth.

SCENE 92
INT. NEWT'S CASE—SHORTLY AFTERWARD—
NIGHT

Jacob holds the Demiguise's hand, leading it through its enclosure.

> NEWT (O.S.)
> Here she comes.

Jacob lifts the Demiguise up and into its nest.

> JACOB
> *(to the Demiguise)*
> Happy to be home? Bet you're
> exhausted, buddy. Come on—
> there you go—that's right.

Tina is tentatively holding the baby Occamy. Supervised by Newt, she places it gently into its nest.

HOLD ON TINA as she looks around at the Erumpent, now stamping through her enclosure. Tina's face is full of wonder and admiration. Jacob chuckles at her expression.

Pickett gives Newt a sharp pinch from inside his pocket.

> NEWT
> Ouch!

Newt fishes Pickett out, holding him up on his hand as he walks through the various enclosures.

We see the Niffler sitting in a small enclave, surrounded by its various treasures.

> NEWT
> Right . . . I think we need to
> talk. See, I wouldn't have let
> him keep you, Pickett. Pick, I
> would rather chop off my hand
> than get rid of you . . . After
> everything you have done for
> me—now come on.

Newt has reached the Thunderbird area.

> NEWT
> Pick—we've talked about
> sulking before, haven't we.
> Pickett—come on, give me a
> smile. Pickett, give me a . . .

Pickett sticks out his tiny tongue and blows a raspberry at Newt.

> NEWT
> All right—now, that is
> beneath you.

Newt places Pickett on his shoulder and starts busying himself with various buckets of feed.

ANGLE ON A PHOTOGRAPH INSIDE NEWT'S SHED,
which shows a beautiful girl—the girl smiles suggestively.
Queenie stares at the photo.

> QUEENIE
> Hey, Newt. Who is she?

> NEWT
> Ah . . . That's no one.

> QUEENIE
> *(reading his mind)*
> Leta Lestrange? I've heard
> of that family. Aren't they
> kinda—you know?

> NEWT
> Please don't read my mind.

A beat as Queenie drinks the whole story out of Newt's head.
She looks both intrigued and saddened. Newt continues to work,
trying hard to pretend Queenie isn't reading his mind.

Queenie steps forward, closer to Newt.

> NEWT
> *(angry, embarrassed)*
> Sorry, I asked you not to.

> QUEENIE
> I know, I'm sorry, I can't help

it. People are easiest to read
when they're hurting.

NEWT

I'm not hurting. Anyway, it
was a long time ago.

QUEENIE

That was a real close friend-
ship you had at school.

NEWT
(attempting to be dismissive)
Yes, well, neither of us really
fitted in at school, so we—

QUEENIE

—became real close. For
years.

*In the background we see Tina, who has noticed that Newt
and Queenie are talking.*

QUEENIE
(concerned)
She was a taker. You need a
giver.

Tina walks toward them.

TINA
What are you two talking about?

NEWT
Ah—nothing.

QUEENIE
School.

NEWT
School.

JACOB
(*putting on his jacket*)
Did you say school? Is there
a school? A wizardry school
here? In America?

QUEENIE
Of course—Ilvermorny! It's
only the best wizard school in
the whole world!

NEWT
I think you'll find the best
wizarding school in the world
is Hogwarts!

QUEENIE
HOGWASH.

A gigantic crack of thunder. The Thunderbird rises into the air screeching, flapping its wings vigorously, its body turning black and gold, its eyes flashing lightning.

Newt stands, examining the bird, concerned.

NEWT
Danger. He senses danger.

SCENE 93
EXT. SECOND SALEM CHURCH—NIGHT

Graves Apparates in the shadows. Wand drawn, he slowly approaches the church, examining the scene of decimation. Rather than nervous, he seems intrigued, almost excited.

SCENE 94
INT. SECOND SALEM CHURCH—NIGHT

The place is destroyed—moonlight filters through gaps in the roof, and Chastity lies dead amid debris from the attack.

Graves slowly enters the church, wand still drawn. Eerie sobbing can be heard from somewhere in the building.

Mary Lou's body lies on the floor in front of him, the marks on her face visible in the moonlight. Graves considers the corpse: a realization dawning on his face—no horror, merely wariness and intense interest.

FOCUS ON CREDENCE, cowering at the back of the church, whimpering and clutching his pendant of the Deathly Hallows. Graves steps quickly toward him, bends down, cradling Credence's head. However, there's little tenderness to his voice as he speaks:

GRAVES
The Obscurial—was here?
Where did she go?

Credence looks up into Graves's face—he is utterly traumatized and unable to explain—his face a plea for affection.

CREDENCE
Help me. Help me.

GRAVES
Didn't you tell me you had
another sister?

Credence begins to weep again. Graves places a hand on his

neck, his face contorting with stress as he tries to remain calm.

                    CREDENCE
          Please help me.

                    GRAVES
          Where's your other sister,
          Credence? The little one?
          Where did she go?

Credence trembles and mumbles.

                    CREDENCE
          Please help me.

Suddenly vicious, Graves slaps Credence hard across the face.

Credence, stunned, stares at Graves.

                    GRAVES
          Your sister's in grave danger.
          We need to find her.

Credence is aghast, unable to comprehend that his hero has hit him. Graves grabs him and pulls him up onto his feet as they Disapparate.

SCENE 95
EXT. TENEMENT IN THE BRONX—NIGHT

A deserted street. Graves, led by Credence, approaches a tenement building.

SCENE 96
INT. TENEMENT IN THE BRONX, HALLWAY— NIGHT

Inside, the building is miserable, dilapidated. Credence and Graves climb the stairwell.

> GRAVES (O.S.)
> What is this place?

> CREDENCE
> Ma adopted Modesty out of
> here. From a family of twelve.
> She still misses her brothers
> and sisters. She still talks
> about them.

Graves, wand in hand, looks around the landing—there are numerous darkened doorways stretching out in several directions.

Credence, still shell-shocked, has stopped in the stairwell.

> GRAVES
> Where is she?

Credence looks down—at a loss.

> CREDENCE
> I don't know.

Graves becomes increasingly impatient—he's so close to his goal. He marches forward into one of the rooms.

> GRAVES
> (*contemptuous*)
> You're a Squib, Credence.
> I could smell it off you the
> minute I met you.

Credence's face falls.

> CREDENCE
> What?

Graves marches back along the corridor to try another room, his pretense of care for Credence all but forgotten.

> GRAVES
> You have magical ancestry,
> but no power.

> CREDENCE
> But you said you could teach
> me—

> GRAVES
> You're unteachable. Your
> mother's dead. That's your
> reward.

Graves points to another landing.

GRAVES
I'm done with you.

*Credence doesn't move. He stares after Graves, his
breathing becoming shallow and quick, as though he's
trying to contain something.*

*Graves moves through the dark rooms. A tiny movement
somewhere close.*

GRAVES
Modesty?

*Graves advances cautiously into a derelict schoolroom at
the end of a corridor.*

SCENE 97
**INT. TENEMENT IN THE BRONX, DERELICT
ROOM—NIGHT**

*ANGLE ON MODESTY cowering in a corner, wide-eyed
with fear and shaking as Graves approaches.*

GRAVES
(*whispering*)
Modesty.

Graves bends down and puts his wand away—once again playing the soothing parent.

GRAVES
(*gentle*)
There's no need to be afraid.
I'm here with your brother,
Credence.

Modesty whimpers with terror at the mention of Credence.

GRAVES
Out you come, now . . .

Graves extends his hand.

A faint jingle sounds.

ANGLE ON THE CEILING as cracks begin to appear, spreading like a spider's web. Dust begins to fall as the walls shake uncontrollably, the room beginning to disintegrate around them.

Graves stands. He looks down at Modesty, but she is clearly terrified and not the source of this magic. Graves turns and slowly draws his wand, the wall in front of him collapsing

as though turned to sand, revealing another wall ahead. Modesty is nothing to him now.

As each wall collapses in front of him, he is transfixed, elated, yet also aware that he has made a colossal error . . .

The final wall collapses. He is facing Credence, who stares at him, unable to control his fury, his sense of betrayal, his bitterness.

> GRAVES
> Credence . . . I owe you an apology . . .

> CREDENCE
> I trusted you. I thought you were my friend. That you were different.

Credence's face begins to contort, his rage tearing him from within.

> GRAVES
> You can control it, Credence.

> CREDENCE
> *(whispers, making eye contact finally)*
> But I don't think I want to, Mr. Graves.

The Obscurus moves horribly beneath Credence's skin. An awful inhuman growl comes out of his mouth, from which something dark begins to bloom.

This force finally takes over Credence, his whole body exploding into a dark mass that hurtles forward out the window, narrowly missing Graves.

Graves stands watching as the Obscurus zooms out and over the city.

SCENE 98
EXT. TENEMENT IN THE BRONX—NIGHT

We follow the Obscurus as it churns and twists through the city, wreaking havoc. Cars are sent flying, pavements explode, and buildings are demolished—the Obscurus leaves only destruction in its wake.

SCENE 99
EXT. SQUIRE'S ROOFTOP—NIGHT

Newt, Tina, Jacob, and Queenie stand on the rooftop underneath a large SQUIRE'S sign. From the edge they have a clear view of the chaos going on below.

> JACOB
> *(overstimulated)*
> Jeez . . . Is that the Obscuria-
> thing?

Sirens sound. Newt is staring, registering the scale of the destruction.

> NEWT
> That's more powerful than
> any Obscurial I have ever
> heard of . . .

A particularly loud explosion in the distance. The city beneath them is starting to burn. Newt thrusts his case into Tina's hands and takes a journal from his pocket.

> NEWT
> If I don't come back,
> look after my creatures.
> Everything that you need to
> know is in there.

He hands her the journal, barely able to make eye contact.

TINA

What?

NEWT
(looking back to the Obscurus)
They're not killing it.

Their eyes meet—a moment full of what they might have said to each other—before Newt jumps from the roof and Disapparates.

TINA
(distraught)
NEWT!

Tina slams the case into Queenie's arms.

TINA
You heard him—look after
them!

Tina also Disapparates. Queenie shoves the case at Jacob.

QUEENIE
Keep holda that, honey.

She moves to Disapparate, but Jacob hangs on to her and she falters.

JACOB

No, no, no!

QUEENIE

I can't take you. Please let go
of me, Jacob!

JACOB

Hey—hey! You're the one
that said I was one of
youse . . . right?

QUEENIE

It's too dangerous.

*A further massive explosion in the distance. Jacob tightens
his grip on Queenie. She reads his mind and her expression
changes to one of wonderment and tenderness as she sees
what he went through in the war. Queenie is moved and
appalled. Very slowly, she raises a hand and touches his
cheek.*

SCENE 100
EXT. TIMES SQUARE—NIGHT

*The scene is one of total chaos. Buildings are on fire, people
scream and run in all directions, cars lie destroyed in the
street.*

*Graves prowls through the square, oblivious to the distress
around him, his focus concentrated on only one thing.*

*The Obscurus writhes at one end of the square, its energy
angrier now—moving through layers of hurt and anguish,
the products of isolation and torment—flecks of red light
roaring from within. Credence's face is just discernible*

within the mass, distorted, pained. Graves stands before it, triumphant.

Newt Apparates from farther down the street and watches.

> GRAVES
> *(shouting to reach Credence*
> *over the almighty noise)*
> To survive so long, with this
> inside you, Credence, is a
> miracle. You are a miracle.
> Come with me—think of
> what we could achieve
> together.

The Obscurus moves closer to Graves—we hear a scream from within the mass as its Dark energy bursts out once more, knocking Graves to the ground. The force sends a shock wave around the square—Newt dives behind a fallen car for cover.

Tina Apparates into the square and takes cover by another burning vehicle close to Newt. They look at each other.

> TINA
> Newt!

> NEWT
> It's the Second Salem boy.
> He's the Obscurial.

TINA
He's not a child.

NEWT
I know—but I saw him—his
power must be so strong—
he's somehow managed to
survive. It's incredible.

As the Obscurus screams once more, Tina makes a decision.

TINA
Newt! Save him.

*Tina dashes out toward Graves. Newt, understanding,
Disapparates.*

SCENE 101
EXT. TIMES SQUARE—NIGHT

*Graves is moving nearer and nearer to the Obscurus, which
continues to scream and wail at his presence. He takes out
his wand, poised . . .*

*Tina runs into view behind Graves. She fires at him, but he
turns just in time, his reactions marvelous, astounding.*

The Obscurus now vanishes. Graves, thoroughly irritated, advances on Tina, deflecting her spells with perfect ease.

> GRAVES
> Tina. You're always turning
> up where you are least
> wanted.

Graves summons an abandoned car, which whooshes through the air, forcing Tina to dive out of the way, just in time.

By the time Tina has gathered herself up from the ground, Graves has Disapparated.

SCENE 102
INT. MAJOR INVESTIGATION DEPARTMENT, MACUSA—NIGHT

A metallic map of New York City lights up to show areas of intense magical activity. Madam Picquery, surrounded by top Aurors, looks on, aghast.

> MADAM PICQUERY
> Contain this, or we are
> exposed and it will mean war.

The Aurors immediately Disapparate.

SCENE 103
EXT. ROOFTOPS OF NEW YORK—NIGHT

Newt race-Apparates as fast as he can across the tops of buildings in pursuit of the Obscurus.

> NEWT
> Credence! Credence, I can
> help you.

The Obscurus dives toward Newt, who Disapparates just in time, before continuing to chase it across the rooftops.

As he runs, spells explode around him, disintegrating the rooftops. A dozen Aurors have appeared, attacking the Obscurus from ahead, and almost taking out Newt, who leaps for cover, trying desperately to keep up.

The Obscurus veers to avoid the spells, leaving black snowlike particles that drift across the rooftops as it retreats, screaming, and turns down another block.

In a particularly vigorous display, the Obscurus now rises dramatically up into the air, as spells in electric blue and

white hit it from all angles. Finally it crashes to the ground and races along a wide, empty street—a black tsunami destroying anything in its path.

SCENE 104
EXT. OUTSIDE A SUBWAY STATION—NIGHT

A line of policemen stand with their guns aimed at the terrifying supernatural force powering toward them.

Their faces turn from confused alarm to total panic as they see the mass swarming ahead, making straight for them. They fire their guns—their efforts futile in the face of such a seemingly unstoppable kinetic mass. Finally they disband, fleeing down the street, just as the Obscurus reaches them.

SCENE 105
EXT. ROOFTOPS/STREETS OF NEW YORK—
NIGHT

*ANGLE ON NEWT, standing on top of a skyscraper
looking out as the Obscurus rises up over the surrounding
buildings and slams spectacularly into the ground just
outside the City Hall subway entrance.*

*Sudden quiet. A pulsing, heavy, screechy breathing
emanates from the Obscurus where it rests at the entrance.*

*Finally, as Newt watches, we see the black mass shrink to
nothing, and the small figure of Credence descends the steps
into the subway.*

SCENE 106
INT. SUBWAY—NIGHT

Newt Apparates into the City Hall subway, a long, mosaicked, Art Deco station tunnel that bears the signs of having been crossed by the Obscurus: The chandelier creaks, a few tiles have fallen. We can hear its deep breathing, cornered, like a frightened panther.

Newt creeps along the platform, trying to find the epicenter of the sound, as the Obscurus slides down the ceiling.

SCENE 107
EXT. SUBWAY ENTRANCE—NIGHT

Aurors surround the entrance to the subway. Pointing their wands at the pavement and into the sky, they draw an invisible energy field around the entrance.

We hear more Aurors arrive, among them Graves—scanning, calculating, and immediately taking charge.

GRAVES
Bar the area. I don't want anyone
else down there!

As the magical field is almost complete, a figure rolls underneath it and dashes unseen into the subway—Tina.

SCENE 108
INT. SUBWAY—NIGHT

Newt has reached the Obscurus in the shadows of a tunnel. Now much calmer, it gently swirls in the air above the train tracks.

Newt hides behind a pillar as he talks.

NEWT
Credence . . . It's Credence,
isn't it? I'm here to help you,
Credence. I'm not here to
hurt you.

In the distance we hear footsteps, the pacing controlled, deliberate.

Newt moves out from behind the pillar and steps onto the train tracks. Within the mass of the Obscurus we can see a shadow of Credence, curled up, scared.

> NEWT
>
> I've met someone just like
> you, Credence. A girl—a
> young girl who'd been
> imprisoned, she had been
> locked away and she'd been
> punished for her magic.

Credence is listening—he never dreamed there was another. Slowly the Obscurus melts away, leaving only Credence, huddled on the train tracks—a frightened child.

Newt crouches on the floor. Credence looks to him, the tiniest trace of hope dawning in his expression: Might there be a way back?

> NEWT
>
> Credence, can I come over to
> you? Can I come over?

Newt slowly moves forward, but as he does so a sharp burst of light blazes out from the darkness and a spell strikes, throwing him backward.

Graves marches down the tunnel with intense purpose.

Credence begins to run as Graves fires further spells at Newt, who rolls out of the way toward the tunnel's central pillars. From here, Newt tries to fire back, but his efforts are easily deflected.

Credence continues to lumber down the tracks but stops—a rabbit caught in the headlights—as a train approaches, its lights glaring from the darkness.

It is up to Graves to save Credence—magically casting him out of the train's path.

SCENE 109
EXT. SUBWAY ENTRANCE—NIGHT

Madam Picquery surveys the situation from under the magical force field.

ANGLE FROM THE CROWD AND POLICE'S POV—
People begin to swarm around the subway, their cries and chatter becoming louder as they stare at the magical bubble surrounding the subway. Reporters have appeared, photographing the scene with an increased frenzy.

Shaw Sr. and Barker push their way through the crowds.

> SHAW SR.
> That thing killed my son—I
> want justice!

CLOSE ON MADAM PICQUERY as she looks out to the crowds.

SHAW SR. (O.S.)
I'll expose you for who you
are and what you've done.

SCENE 110
INT. SUBWAY—NIGHT

Graves stands on the platform, continuing to duel with Newt, who stands on the train tracks. Credence cowers behind him.

Finally, almost bored by Newt's efforts, Graves casts a spell that ripples along the train tracks and down the tunnel, finally blasting into Newt, throwing him high into the air.

Newt lands on his back and Graves immediately sets upon him, casting spells in a whiplike motion with increasing vigor. Graves's immense power is evident, as Newt writhes on the ground, unable to stop him.

SCENE 111
EXT. SUBWAY ENTRANCE—NIGHT

WIDE SHOT—we see the luminous wall of vibrating energy now flashing with the power of the magic it contains.

Langdon, drunk, stares, enthralled and amazed with the spectacle.

> SHAW SR.
> *(to the photographers
> around him)*
> Look! Take photos!

SCENE 112
INT. SUBWAY—NIGHT

Graves continues to whip Newt, a manic, crazed look in his eyes.

*CLOSE ON CREDENCE, farther down the tunnel,
sobbing. He begins to shake, his face slowly turning black as
he tries to stop the kinetic mass from rising up within him.*

*As Newt cries out in pain, Credence succumbs to the
blackness—his body enveloped and overcome—the
Obscurus rising up and blasting down the tunnel toward
Graves.*

*Graves is mesmerized—he falls to his knees beneath the
vast black mass—pleading in wonder.*

GRAVES
Credence.

*The Obscurus lets out an unearthly scream and dives
toward Graves, who Disapparates just in time. The
Obscurus continues to blast around the tunnel.*

*Graves and Newt Disapparate and Apparate around the
subway, trying to avoid the Obscurus's path. This causes
the station to disintegrate even faster. Suddenly the force
accelerates, becoming a giant wave that consumes the entire
space before flying out through the roof.*

SCENE 113
EXT. SUBWAY ENTRANCE—NIGHT

The Obscurus crashes up through the pavement, watched by wizards and No-Majs alike. It storms up a half-built skyscraper, windows shattering at every level, electric wiring exploding, until it reaches the skeletal framework of scaffolding above, which buckles perilously.

Below it, the crowd outside the magical cordon runs for cover, terrified.

The Obscurus forms a wide disc shape before plunging back down into the subway.

SCENE 114
INT. SUBWAY—NIGHT

The Obscurus screams and dives, bursting through the subway roof—for a split second, both Newt and Graves seem on the point of death—as they lie on the tracks, cowering beneath this Dark force.

TINA (O.S.)

CREDENCE, NO!

Tina runs onto the tracks.

Inches from Graves's face, the Obscurus freezes. Slowly, very slowly, it rises back up, swirling more gently, staring at Tina, who looks straight back into its weird eyes.

TINA
Don't do this—please.

NEWT
Keep talking, Tina. Keep
talking to him—he'll listen to
you. He's listening.

Inside the Obscurus, Credence reaches out to Tina, the only person who has ever done him an uncomplicated kindness. He looks at Tina, desperate and afraid. He has dreamed of her ever since she saved him from a beating.

TINA
I know what that woman did
to you . . . I know that you've
suffered . . . You need to stop
this now . . . Newt and I will
protect you . . .

Graves is on his feet.

TINA
(*pointing to Graves*)
This man—he is using you.

GRAVES
Don't listen to her, Credence.
I want you to be free. It's all
right.

TINA
(*to Credence, calming him*)
That's it . . .

The Obscurus is beginning to shrink. Its dreadful face is becoming more human, more like Credence's own.

Suddenly Aurors begin pouring down the steps of the subway and into the tunnel. More Aurors advance from behind Tina, their wands raised aggressively.

TINA
Shhh! Don't, you'll frighten
him.

The Obscurus lets out a terrible moan and begins to swell again. The station is crumbling. Newt and Tina wheel around, arms akimbo, both trying to protect Credence.

Graves spins to face the Aurors, wand at the ready.

GRAVES
        Wands down! Anyone harms
        him—they'll answer to me—
            (turning back to Credence)
        Credence!

                     TINA
        Credence . . .

The Aurors begin pelting the Obscurus with spells.

                    GRAVES
        NO!

*We see Credence from within the black mass, his face
contorted, screaming. The barrage of spells continues and
Credence howls in pain.*

SCENE 115
EXT. SUBWAY ENTRANCE—NIGHT

*The magical force field surrounding the subway breaks
down as people continue to flee the scene. Only Shaw Sr.
and Langdon stand steadfast, captivated.*

SCENE 116
INT. SUBWAY—NIGHT

Aurors continue to aim spells at the Obscurus, their efforts unrelenting and brutal.

Under this pressure, the Obscurus finally seems to implode—a white ball of magical light taking over from the black mass.

The force of the change sends Tina, Newt, and the Aurors stumbling backward.

All power subsides. Only small tatters of black matter are left—floating through the air like feathers.

Newt gets to his feet, his face racked with deep-felt grief. Tina remains on the floor, crying.

Graves, however, climbs up, back onto the platform, as close as possible to the remnants of the black mass.

The Aurors advance toward Graves.

GRAVES
You fools. Do you realize
what you've done?

Graves seethes as the others watch him with interest.
Madam Picquery emerges from behind the Aurors, her tone
steely, questioning.

MADAM PICQUERY
The Obscurial was killed on
my orders, Mr. Graves.

GRAVES
Yes. And history will surely
note that, Madam President.

Graves moves toward her along the platform, his tone
threatening.

GRAVES
What was done here tonight
was not right!

MADAM PICQUERY
He was responsible for
the death of a No-Maj. He
risked the exposure of our
community. He has broken
one of our most sacred laws—

GRAVES
(laughing bitterly)
A law that has us scuttling
like rats in the gutter! A
law that demands that we
conceal our true nature! A
law that directs those under
its dominion to cower in fear
lest we risk discovery! I ask
you, Madam President—
(eyes flashing to all present)
—I ask all of you—who does
this law protect? Us?
(gesturing vaguely to the
No-Majs above)
Or them?
(smiling bitterly)
I refuse to bow down any
longer.

Graves walks away from the Aurors.

MADAM PICQUERY
(to the Aurors flanking her)
Aurors, I'd like you to relieve
Mr. Graves of his wand and
escort him back to—

As Graves moves down the platform, a wall of white light
suddenly appears in front of him, blocking his path.

Graves thinks for a moment—a sneer of derision and irritation crossing his face. He turns.

Graves strides confidently back along the platform, firing spells at both groups of Aurors facing him. Spells fly back at him from all angles, but Graves parries them all. Several Aurors are sent flying—Graves appears to be winning . . .

In a split second, Newt pulls the cocoon from his pocket and releases it at Graves. The Swooping Evil soars around him, shielding Newt and the Aurors from Graves's spells, and giving Newt time to raise his wand.

With a sense that he's been holding this one back, he slashes it through the air: Out flies a crackling rope of supernatural light that wraps itself around Graves like a whip. Graves tries to hold it off as it tightens, but staggers, struggles, and falls to his knees, dropping his wand.

TINA

    Accio.

Graves's wand flies into Tina's hand. Graves looks around at them, a deep hatred in his eyes.

Newt and Tina slowly advance, Newt raising his wand.

NEWT

    Revelio.

Graves transforms. He is no longer dark, but blond and blue-eyed. He is the man on the posters. A murmur spreads through the crowd: GRINDELWALD.

Madam Picquery moves toward him.

> GRINDELWALD
> *(with contempt)*
> Do you think *you* can hold
> me?

> MADAM PICQUERY
> We'll do our best, Mr.
> Grindelwald.

Grindelwald stares intently at Madam Picquery, his expression of disgust turning into a small, derisory smile. He is forced to his feet by two Aurors, who move him toward the entrance.

As Grindelwald reaches Newt, he pauses—both smiling and sneering.

> GRINDELWALD
> Will we die, just a little?

He is led away, up and out of the subway. Newt watches, bemused.

TIME CUT:

Queenie and Jacob push their way through to the front of the Aurors. Jacob holds Newt's case.

Queenie hugs Tina. Newt stares at Jacob.

> JACOB
> Hey . . . I figured somebody
> oughta keep an eye on this
> thing.

He hands Newt his case.

> NEWT
> *(humble, completely grateful)*
> Thank you.

Madam Picquery addresses the group as she stares through the broken roof of the subway station, into the world outside.

> MADAM PICQUERY
> We owe you an apology, Mr.
> Scamander. But the magical
> community is exposed! We
> cannot Obliviate an entire
> city.

A beat as this sinks in.

As Newt follows Madam Picquery's gaze, he sees a tendril of black matter, a small part of the Obscurus, floating down through the roof. Unnoticed by anyone else, it eventually floats up and away, trying to reconnect with its host.

A pause. Newt's attention snaps back to the problem at hand.

NEWT
Actually, I think we can.

TIME CUT:

Newt has placed his case wide-open underneath the huge hole in the subway roof.

CLOSE ON NEWT'S OPEN CASE.

Suddenly the Thunderbird bursts forth in a flurry of feathers and gushes of wind—the crowd of Aurors backs away. The creature is beautiful, mesmerizing but scary, as he flaps his powerful wings and hovers above them.

Newt moves forward—he examines Frank, a look of real tenderness and pride on his face.

NEWT
I was intending to wait until
we got to Arizona, but it
seems like now you are our
only hope, Frank.

A look between them—an understanding. Newt reaches out his arm, and Frank presses his beak lovingly into the embrace—they nuzzle each other affectionately.

The assembled group watches in awe.

NEWT
I'll miss you too.

Newt steps back, taking the flask of Swooping Evil venom from his pocket.

NEWT
(to the Thunderbird)
You know what you've got to
do.

Newt throws the vial high up into the air—Frank lets out a sharp cry, catching it in his beak and immediately soaring out of the subway.

SCENE 117
EXT. NEW YORK—SKY—DAWN

No-Majs and Aurors alike shriek and recoil as the magnificent Thunderbird bursts forth from the subway, gliding into the dawn-lit sky.

We follow the Thunderbird as he rises higher and higher into the air. As his wings flap harder, faster, storm clouds congregate. Lightning flashes. We spiral upward as the Thunderbird twists and turns, leaving New York lying far below.

CLOSE ON FRANK'S BEAK, the vial clutched tightly and finally crushed. The powerful venom spreads through the thick rain, enchanting it, thickening it. The darkening sky flashes a brilliant blue and rain begins to fall.

SCENE 118
EXT. SUBWAY ENTRANCE—DAWN

HIGH ANGLE pushing down toward the crowd as they look up to the sky. As the rain falls and hits them, people move on, docile—their bad memories washed away. Each

person goes about their daily business as though nothing unusual has happened.

Aurors move through the streets, performing Repairing Charms to rebuild the city: Buildings and cars are reconstructed and streets are returned to normal.

ANGLE ON LANGDON, standing in the rain, his expression softening, growing blank as the water runs over his face.

ANGLE ON POLICE looking at their guns, confused— why do they have them drawn? They slowly gather themselves, putting their weapons away.

Inside a small family home, a young mother looks on fondly at her family. As she takes a sip of water, her expression becomes blank.

Groups of Aurors continue to repair the streets, swiftly reassembling broken tram tracks, all traces of destruction finally disappearing. One Auror, passing a newsstand, enchants the papers, removing Newt's and Tina's mug shots and replacing them with banal headlines about the weather.

Mr. Bingley, the bank manager, stands in his bathroom taking a shower. As the water trickles over him, he too is Obliviated. We see Bingley's wife, brushing her teeth, her expression vacant, carefree.

*The Thunderbird continues to soar through the streets of
New York, churning up more and more rain as he goes, his
feathers shimmering a brilliant gold. Finally he glides into
the breaking New York dawn, a magnificent sight.*

SCENE 119
INT. SUBWAY PLATFORM—DAWN

*As Madam Picquery looks on, the roof of the subway is
swiftly repaired.*

Newt addresses the group:

> NEWT
> They won't remember
> anything. That venom
> has incredibly powerful
> Obliviative properties.

> MADAM PICQUERY
> *(impressed)*
> We owe you a great debt, Mr.
> Scamander. Now—get that
> case out of New York.

NEWT
Yes, Madam President.

Madam Picquery begins to walk away, her pack of Aurors moving with her. Suddenly she turns back. Queenie, having read her mind, stands protectively in front of Jacob, trying to hide him.

MADAM PICQUERY
Is that No-Maj still here?
(on seeing Jacob)
Obliviate him. There can be
no exceptions.

Madam Picquery reads the anguish in their faces.

MADAM PICQUERY
I'm sorry—but even one
witness . . . you know the law.

A pause. She is uncomfortable at their distress.

MADAM PICQUERY
I'll let you say good-bye.

She leaves.

SCENE 120
EXT. SUBWAY—DAWN

Jacob leads the others up the steps of the subway, Queenie following close behind him.

Rain is still falling heavily, the streets now almost empty but for a few hardworking Aurors.

Jacob has reached the top of the steps and stands gazing into the rain. Queenie reaches out and grabs his coat, willing him not to move out into the street. Jacob turns to her.

JACOB

Hey. Hey, this is for the best.
(off their looks)
Yeah—I was—I was never
even supposed to be here.

Jacob fights back tears. Queenie gazes up at him, her beautiful face full of distress. Tina and Newt, too, look incredibly sad.

JACOB

I was never supposed to
know any of this. Everybody
knows Newt only kept me
around because—hey—Newt,
why did you keep me around?

Newt has to be explicit. It doesn't come easily.

NEWT

Because I like you. Because
you're my friend and I'll
never forget how you helped
me, Jacob.

A beat.

Jacob is overcome with emotion at Newt's answer.

JACOB

Oh!

*Queenie moves forward up the stairs toward Jacob—they
stand close.*

QUEENIE
(*trying to cheer him up*)
I'll come with you. We'll
go somewhere—we'll go

anywhere—see, I ain't never
gonna find anyone like—

> JACOB
> (*bravely*)
> There's loads like me.

> QUEENIE
> No ... No ... There's only
> one like you.

The pain is almost unbearable.

> JACOB
> (*a beat*)
> I gotta go.

Jacob turns to face the rain, and wipes his eyes.

> NEWT
> (*starting after him*)
> JACOB!

> JACOB
> (*trying to smile*)
> It's okay ... It's okay ... It's
> okay. It's just like waking up,
> right?

The group smiles back at him, encouraging, trying to soothe the situation.

Looking at their faces as he moves, Jacob walks backward into the rain. Turning his face to the sky, arms out, he allows the water to wash over him completely.

Queenie creates a magical umbrella with her wand and steps out toward Jacob. She moves in close, tenderly stroking Jacob's face before closing her eyes and bending in to gently kiss him.

Finally she pulls slowly away, her gaze not leaving Jacob's face even for a second. Then, suddenly, she's gone, leaving Jacob standing, arms out, longingly embracing no one.

CLOSE ON JACOB'S FACE as he fully "wakes up," blank faced and confused by his location and the torrential downpour he's standing in. He finally moves off through the streets—a lonely figure.

SCENE 121
EXT. JACOB'S CANNING FACTORY—A WEEK
LATER—EARLY EVENING

An exhausted Jacob, surrounded by a crowd of similarly overalled production line workers, is leaving after a hard day's shift. He carries a battered leather case.

A man walks toward him—Newt. They collide and Jacob's case is knocked to the ground.

NEWT

So sorry—sorry!

Newt has moved swiftly and purposefully onward.

JACOB

(no recognition)

Hey!

*Jacob bends to pick up his case and looks down, puzzled.
His old case is suddenly very heavy. One of the catches
flicks open of its own accord. Jacob smiles a little, and bends
down to open the case.*

*Inside, the case is filled with solid silver Occamy eggshells, a
note attached. As Jacob reads, we hear:*

NEWT (V.O.)

*Dear Mr. Kowalski, You are
wasted in a canning factory.
Please take these Occamy
eggshells as collateral for your
bakery. A well-wisher.*

SCENE 122
EXT. NEW YORK HARBOR—NEXT DAY

*CLOSE ON NEWT'S FEET as he walks through the
crowds.*

*Newt is preparing to leave New York, overcoat on, Hufflepuff
scarf around his neck, case tied up tightly with string.*

*Tina walks alongside him. They stop before the boarding
gate. Tina looks anxious.*

NEWT
(*smiling*)
Well, it's been . . .

TINA
Hasn't it!

Pause. Newt looks up, Tina's expression is expectant.

TINA
Listen, Newt, I wanted to
thank you.

NEWT
What on earth for?

TINA
Well, you know, if you hadn't
said all those nice things to
Madam Picquery about me—I
wouldn't be back on the
investigative team now.

NEWT
Well—I can't think of
anyone that I'd rather have
investigating me.

Not precisely what he was aiming for, but too late now . . .
Newt becomes slightly awkward, Tina shyly appreciative.

TINA
Well, try not to need
investigating for a bit.

NEWT
I will. Quiet life for me
from now on . . . back
to the Ministry . . . deliver
my manuscript . . .

TINA
I'll look out for it. *Fantastic
Beasts and Where to Find Them.*

Weak smiles. A pause. Tina plucks up courage.

TINA
Does Leta Lestrange like to
read?

NEWT
Who?

TINA
The girl whose picture you
carry—

NEWT
I don't really know what

Leta likes these days because
people change.

TINA

Yes.

NEWT
(*a dawning realization*)
I've changed. I think. Maybe
a little.

Tina is delighted, but doesn't know how to express it.
Instead, she's trying not to cry. The ship's siren sounds—
most of the other passengers have now boarded.

NEWT
I'll send you a copy of my
book, if I may.

TINA
I'd like that.

Newt gazes at Tina—awkwardly affectionate. He gently
reaches forward and touches her hair. Lingering for a
moment, they stare into each other's eyes.

A last look and Newt suddenly moves away, leaving Tina
standing, raising a hand to touch where Newt stroked her hair.

But then he's back.

NEWT
I'm so sorry—how would you
feel if I gave you your copy in
person?

A radiant smile breaks across Tina's face.

TINA
I'd like that—very much.

*Newt can't help but grin back at her before turning and
walking away.*

*He pauses on the gangplank, perhaps unsure of how to act,
but eventually moves on without looking back.*

*Tina stands alone in the empty harbor. As she walks away,
there's a playful skip to her step.*

SCENE 123
EXT. JACOB'S BAKERY, LOWER EAST SIDE—
THREE MONTHS LATER—DAY

WIDE SHOT OF A BUSTLING NEW YORK STREET—
market stalls line the street, which heaves with busy people,
horses, and carriages.

ANGLE ON A SMALL, INVITING BAKERY—crowds
throng outside the pretty little shop, painted with the name:
KOWALSKI. *People peer with interest into the shop's windows,*
and happy customers leave, their arms laden with baked
goods.

SCENE 124
INT. JACOB'S BAKERY, LOWER EAST SIDE—
DAY

CLOSE ON THE DOORBELL as it rings to signal the entrance of a new customer.

CLOSE ON THE PASTRIES AND BREADS on the counter, all molded into fanciful little shapes—we recognize the Demiguise, Niffler, and Erumpent among them.

Jacob, serving, is very happy, his shop full to bursting with customers.

> FEMALE CUSTOMER
> (*examining the little*
> *pastries*)
> Where do you get your ideas
> from, Mr. Kowalski?

> JACOB
> I don't know, I don't know—
> they just come!

He hands the lady her pastries.

> JACOB
> Here you go—don't forget
> this—enjoy.

Jacob turns and calls over one of his bakery assistants, handing him a pair of keys.

> JACOB
> Hey, Henry—storage, all
> right? Thanks, pal.

The bell tinkles again.

Jacob looks up and is thunderstruck all over again: It's Queenie. They stare at each other—Queenie beams, radiant. Jacob, quizzical and totally enchanted, touches his neck—a flicker of memory. He smiles back.

THE
END

ACKNOWLEDGMENTS

Without the patience and wisdom of Steve Kloves and David Yates, there would be no Fantastic Beasts screenplay. They have my boundless gratitude for every note, every piece of encouragement, every improvement they suggested. Learning, in Steve's immortal words, to "fit the woman to the dress" has been a fascinating, challenging, exasperating, exhilarating, infuriating, and ultimately rewarding experience that I wouldn't have missed for the world. I couldn't have done it without them.

David Heyman has been with me from the very first step of Harry Potter's transition to the big screen, and Fantastic Beasts would have been immeasurably poorer without him. It's been a very long journey since that first queasy lunch in Soho, and he is currently bringing to Newt all the knowledge, dedication, and expertise that he brought to Harry Potter.

There would never have been a Fantastic Beasts franchise without Kevin Tsujihara. Even though I've been carrying the germ of the idea for Fantastic Beasts since 2001, when I wrote the initial book for charity, it took Kevin to make me commit to bringing Newt's story to the big screen. His support has been

283

invaluable and he deserves the lion's share of the credit for making this happen.

Last, but never least, my family have been enormously supportive of this project even though it has meant me working through a year's worth of vacations. I don't know where I'd be without you, except that it would be a dark and lonely place where I wouldn't feel like inventing anything. So, to Neil, Jessica, David, and Kenzie: Thank you for being completely wonderful, funny, and loving, and for still believing that I should pursue Fantastic Beasts, however tricky and time-consuming they may sometimes be.

GLOSSARY OF FILM TERMS

Back to scene—After focusing on one character or action within a scene, the camera returns to the larger scene

Close on—The camera films a person or object from close range

Ext.—*Exterior*; an outside location

Flash cut—An extremely brief transition shot, sometimes as short as one frame

High wide—The camera is placed above, "looking down" on the subject or scene from a wide angle

Hold on—The camera rests on a person or object

Int.—*Interior*; an indoor location

Jump cut—Cutting from one important moment to the next from the same angle. This transition is usually used to show a very brief time-lapse.

Montage—A series of shots in a sequence condensing space, time, and information, often with music accompanying it

O.S.—*Off-screen*; action that takes place off-screen or dialogue that is spoken without seeing the character on-screen

POV—*Point of view*; the camera films from a particular character's point of view

Pan—Camera movement involving the camera turning on a stationary axis moving slowly from one subject to another

Sotto voce—Spoken at a whisper or under one's breath

Time cut—Cutting to later in the same scene

V.O.—*Voice-over*; dialogue spoken by a character not present in the scene on-screen

Wide shot—The camera shows the entire object or human figure, usually intended to place it in some relation to its surroundings. It is often used to set the scene of the film.

CAST & CREW

Warner Bros. Pictures Presents
A Heyday Films Production
A David Yates Film

FANTASTIC BEASTS AND WHERE TO FIND THEM

Directed by . . . . David Yates

Written by . . . . .J.K. Rowling

Produced by . . . . . . David Heyman, P.G.A., J.K. Rowling, P.G.A., Steve Kloves, P.G.A., Lionel Wigram, P.G.A.

Executive Producers. . . . . Tim Lewis, Neil Blair, Rick Senat

Director of Photography . . . . . . .Philippe Rousselot, A.F.C./ASC

Production Designer. . . . . .Stuart Craig

Editor . . . . Mark Day

Costume Designer. . . . . Colleen Atwood

Music . . . . James Newton Howard

STARRING

Newt Scamander . . . . Eddie Redmayne

Tina Goldstein . . . . Katherine Waterston

Jacob Kowalski . . . . Dan Fogler

Queenie Goldstein . . . . Alison Sudol

Credence Barebone. . . . . .Ezra Miller

Mary Lou Barebone . . . . Samantha Morton

Henry Shaw Sr. . . . . Jon Voight

Seraphina Picquery. . . . . Carmen Ejogo

and

Percival Graves . . . . Colin Farrell

ABOUT THE AUTHOR

J.K. Rowling is the author of the bestselling Harry Potter series of seven books, published between 1997 and 2007, which have sold over 450 million copies worldwide, are distributed in more than 200 territories and translated into 79 languages, and have been turned into eight blockbuster films by Warner Bros. She has written three companion volumes to the series in aid of charity: *Quidditch Through the Ages* and *Fantastic Beasts and Where to Find Them* in aid of Comic Relief, and *The Tales of Beedle the Bard* in aid of her children's charity Lumos. Her website and e-publisher, Pottermore, is the digital hub of the Wizarding World. She collaborated with writer Jack Thorne and director John Tiffany on the stage play *Harry Potter and the Cursed Child Parts One and Two*, which premiered in 2016 in London's West End. J.K. Rowling is also the author of a novel for adult readers, *The Casual Vacancy*, and, under the pseudonym Robert Galbraith, is the author of three crime novels featuring private detective Cormoran Strike, which are to be adapted for BBC television. *Fantastic Beasts and Where to Find Them* is J.K. Rowling's first screenplay.

ABOUT THE BOOK DESIGN

This book was designed by MinaLima, an award-winning design studio founded by Miraphora Mina and Eduardo Lima, who were graphic designers on *Fantastic Beasts and Where to Find Them* and on the eight Harry Potter films.

The cover and illustrations in this book were based on creatures in the story and inspired by 1920s decorative style. They were drawn by hand and finished digitally in Adobe Illustrator. The text was set in Crimson Text, and the display type was set in Sheridan Gothic SG.